Westbound Awakening

USA TODAY BESTSELLING AUTHOR
HILDIE MCQUEEN

PINK
DOOR
PUBLISHING

Westbound Awakening

Pink Door Publishing

Cover Artist: Dar Albert, Wicked Smart Designs
Editor: Scott Moreland

The characters and events portrayed in this book are fictitious. Any similarity to real persons, living or dead, is purely coincidental and not intended by the author.

DEDICATION AND ACKNOWLEDGEMENTS

I would like to express my sincerest appreciation to my readers who have supported me every single step of this amazing journey. I am truly blessed to have each of you in my life.

A special acknowledgement to the wonderful Sheila Mast for final edits on this book. You have a kind heart. Thank you!

An unforgettable journey…

Captain John McClain finds himself on the wrong end of a shotgun when attempting to find his child. Heading west to find the mother of his son and the outlaw who shot him, John is forced to escort an enticing woman whose lifestyle goes against his moral standards, yet she calls to every part of him.

Heading west to meet the dying father she never knew, and possibly starting a new life, Mae Hawkins didn't expect the added complication of traveling with the one man she always loved.

When they're joined along the road by a minister and his wife, things get beyond complicated for John and Mae who awaken to the lesson that sometimes differences are more imagined than real.

Chapter One

Rage filled eyes met his. The man's hand trembled more from fear than from hatred. It was more than crystal clear the outlaw was not about to wait to find out the reason the Calvary captain came there. The boom of a gunshot echoed in John's ears, the burning penetrated his right leg, and before he could turn away, a second shot sent him to the ground.

Two weeks later, Widow's Peak, Virginia

CAPTAIN JOHN MCCLAIN shook his head to dislodge the thoughts of that fate-filled night. The all too familiar throbbing pulsed down his leg, and he rubbed a palm over his thigh, fingers skimming over the bandaged area under the thick dungarees he wore. Although the wince that surfaced couldn't be helped, John disregarded it. From the corner where he sat, it was easy to keep a vigil on all the exits, and with his back protected, he continued to keep a watchful eye on his men. Every one of the eight tables in the room were surrounded by patrons while vibrantly dressed girls circled the space, beacons of promise much like the first rays of sunshine assuring a fresh start.

The expansive bar along the back of the room manned by a

huge man named James held whiskey bottles of many types that sparkled, reflecting the lights. Several men leaned elbows on the highly sheened counter, drinks in hand.

One of his young soldiers caught his attention. The boy climbed up the brothel's stairs, his hand in one of the establishment's girls. The soldier must have sensed his gaze because hesitant eyes looked over toward him, a wide grin in place. John nodded, and it was the only encouragement the young man needed before he raced up the stairs pulling his prize behind him.

It was a lively night at Mae's Brothel, or perhaps a normal night for all John knew as he'd only been here twice during the evenings. He'd been here plenty of times over the years in the late morning after one of his men failed to show up for duty. It looked so different at night, the gas lamps providing a complementary atmosphere to the darkened interior.

Although windows were open, the meager breeze offered little respite to the heated interior. Pain and lack of visual focus brought him back to his own situation. He blinked in an attempt to will away dizziness caused by the combination of voices, piano music and cigar smoke. Even a deep drink of cold beer did not help.

Hindsight being twenty-twenty and all that, he should have listened to the camp's doctor and taken better care of himself in the beginning. The physician insisted he take time off, allow his leg to heal fully and even ordered him to bed rest for a week. Headstrong, John did not take even one full day. Instead John dragged himself from bed and kept up with his men, riding long days in the heat, pushing away the pain and nausea.

The way he saw it, since he'd been shot while off duty, it was his mistake so his men shouldn't have to pay for it by pulling extra shifts.

When a new jolt of ache trailed up his leg from calf to thigh, John considered that perhaps he should visit the doc again. Although he'd cleaned his wounds himself daily to avoid infection, it could be that he'd not be thorough enough. Something was definitely wrong.

In less than a month, he would no longer be a member of the Confederate cavalry; most of the unit was already disbanded, either going back to their prior lives or moving west to join the established cavalry units. In a few days time, he'd be headed west for a different reason. To find the damn man who'd shot him. This was definitely not the time for him, who generally of good health, to be feverish, dizzy and lacking of energy.

The perfume of honeysuckle freshened the surrounding air, and he inhaled the calming scent.

"Why Captain McClain, it's nice of you to join us tonight. What do I owe the rare honor of your presence to?" The madam, Mae Hawkins' husky voice fell over him like a much-needed cool breeze. He looked up to meet her bright green eyes and lost his ability to speak.

A more beautiful woman did not exist, he would bet his life on it. The woman was like a goddess who deemed to walk amongst mere mortals. The blonde brothel owner cocked an eyebrow at his lack of response.

"Good evening Mae, you look well rested." He almost smiled at the slight frown, her perfectly shaped eyebrows connecting; she was probably used to more elaborate flattery from men. He continued unabated. "I am here to keep an eye on my men. Last time I allowed them to come without supervision, I had to fetch them the next day."

Shoulders back, she fanned her face and eyed him from beneath long lashes, her comely mouth pursed. With hair up in a complicated manner that allowed for some of the long blonde curls to escape and touch her shoulders, she was captivating. Enticing.

"Yes I remember." Mae lowered herself to the chair across from him and allowed her gaze to sweep over the room, always vigilant.

He followed her line of sight to two of his men engrossed with a curvy brunette who threw her head back in laughter, seeming to enjoy the game of pitting them against each other.

Not able to tear his gaze from Mae for long, he studied her, admiring the graceful curve of her neck, the soft jawline and the slight pout of pink lips.

She turned back and smiled, her eyes connecting with his. "They're good boys, most of them. Some nights they just drink too much and can't make it out the door, much less mount. I won't stand for them to leave in that condition. It's dangerous out there if they get lost. I'd rather their stern commander come for them than find out they've met with harm."

Stern? John didn't reply instead took another drink from his now warming beer and gave her a noncommittal shrug. Feigning disinterest, he studied her attire. Although the deep green dress was off her shoulders, very little of her cleavage was exposed. Unlike the other women in the brothel, he'd never seen her wear anything indecent. The few times he'd spotted her out in town, she always dressed within the bounds of modesty. Even so, she commanded attention, a beautiful woman without ties living without the restraints of society.

Her kohl-lined eyes slid toward the back hallway, and he wondered if she took customers. Perhaps as the Madam, she didn't have to work any longer, unless she chose too. Or then again, she could have private lovers. Hell, her beauty alone brought men to their knees so that she did not have to entice them with scant dressing. For some reason the thought of her bedding men made his stomach clench.

He shifted in his seat uncomfortable under her returned scrutiny.

Finally her cool eyes turned to him. "Enjoy your night John," her lips curved at his scowl. She always enjoyed his discomfort at her using his proper name. Mae waved at the beefy bartender. "James, serve Captain McClain another one on the house."

Each movement graceful, Mae rose and went toward the back of the room toward the hallway. Although seeming to glide across the floor, the sway of her hips beckoned every male's attention in the saloon to follow her movements.

When an older man with a cigar hanging precariously from his lips reached to touch her bottom, she slapped it away without turning to look, which brought the other men at his table to burst into laughter.

"Come on Mae, have some pity on my poor soul," the man cried after her. She gifted him with a smile, and he clutched at his chest in a comical response. Mae Hawkins commanded the brothel with a gentle ease that belied a firm hold.

Heated, John tugged at the collar of his shirt. The fever was not fading. If anything, he felt warmer now. No denying it any longer. He would go directly to see the doc at the camp upon his return.

A woman, Lucinda, if he remembered correctly, sat at the piano and began to sing a melancholy tune that fell over the room like a cooling breeze. The beauty of the woman's throaty voice amazed John, and he couldn't help but lean forward to listen. Even the drunks quieted at her song of sorry and loss. He could relate to the words as uninvited visions of the past years, alone with only his men for company, began to appear in his mind, one after another.

Without notice, the walls began to close in, and the room swayed. John lifted his drink and held the cool glass against the side of his face the relief was slight. At the small reprieve, John decided it was best to get some fresh air. If he continued to feel badly once outside, then he'd to head back to camp. His men would in all probability not notice his absence. With a deep breath, he got to his feet and his balance, though precarious, seemed to hold. Grateful to be somewhat steady on his legs, John walked across the room toward the hallway that lead to the kitchens at the back of the house, where his horse was tethered.

Once he exited the crowded room, the air was immediately cooler making it easier to breathe.

"Go back to the saloon Butch and leave me be," Mae's harsh whispered words made John stop, and he squinted into the darkness. The outline of two people filled the darkened hallway, Mae against the wall, a man's arms on both sides of shoulders palms flat on the surface.

The man, whom John recognized as Butch Mason, a local banker, leaned in as if to kiss Mae. He noted that her hands were pressed against Mason's chest, but with the dimness it was hard to tell if she welcomed the male or not. Just in case the attention was unwarranted, John cleared his throat.

Mason swung toward him, his reddened eyes meeting John's for a second before training them back to Mae. "I'll leave you be for now Mae, but I'll be back don't you worry." The man caressed her cheek before sauntering past John without a word.

Releasing a deep exhale, Mae remained against the wall without looking at him. Her hand shook slightly when she reached up, her fingers pushing the golden strands into place.

With mechanical moves, she pushed away from the wall and went to brush past John. "Excuse me."

He reached out and touched her arm. "Are you all right?"

Flat eyes met his, the proud visage reappearing. "I can take care of myself John," Mae replied, her head held high. When he reached for her again, she leaned away from his touch. "You worry about your men and let me worry about mine." The light floral fragrance tickled his nose as she swept past toward the saloon.

No need to go after her. She'd not speak to him about it and rightly so. This was her domain so he continued down the hallway.

The night beckoned, and John walked through the large kitchen to the back door. He pulled it open and stepped through with desperation. When the cool evening air hit his face, John closed his eyes at the relief from the sweltering interior.

Finding comfort in the solitude, he allowed his body to slump against the back porch column. He'd always preferred the freedom of the outdoors, preferring the quiet and stillness to being cloistered indoors. The silence of the moonlit night was broken only by the muddled sounds from inside the house. The moment gave him a welcome relief to the throbbing at his temples. Hands in his pockets, he walked off the back porch and looked up to the star-filled sky. The stars twinkled in a vivid display, and he turned in a full circle until finding the telltale sign of Orion's belt then followed it to outline his favorite constellation. It was several minutes before he tore his eyes from it, the night sky never failing to fascinate him.

When he turned to go back inside and took a couple of steps, the dizziness returned full force. John blinked repeatedly and shook his head in an attempt to get his balance. Just as he reached for the porch railing, his knees buckled from under him, and he slammed to the ground. His head smashed into the packed dirt with force, and he moaned. When his stomach lurched, John took deep breaths to keep from vomiting and rolled to his back. *What the hell just happened?*

The horse's whinnies became softer, and the breeze cooled even more as everything shifted sideways. He was in trouble, needing to get back into the house. With all the strength he could muster, John pushed to sit, but his arms gave out and fell back again.

Next, John attempted to whistle for his horse; with his

parched mouth it impossible. Wetting his lips, he finally did. The beast turned toward him, but his tie prevented it from coming closer. "Damn it," John cursed, then called out through a clenched jaw. "Can anyone hear me?"

Please don't let Mae find me like this. He pushed up again using his arms and legs. Pain seared through his injured leg, and it was too much to bear, so he groaned and fell back once.

The stars overhead began to blur, and he closed his eyes.

Chapter Two

MAE RETURNED TO the saloon and went directly to stand by the bar where she could keep an eye on everything that went on. Thankfully Butch Mason had rejoined a poker game and was oblivious to her, instead concentrating on the cards he held. The middle-aged man was a power to be reckoned with in the town. He served as the town's banker, one of his less obscure dealings. On more than one occasion he'd demanded she invite him to her bed, and when she turned him down, he threatened to take the brothel from her. Although she owned the property free and clear, she had no delusions that if Mason set his mind to it, he could find a way to do it. It worried her that as time passed, he became more and more demanding. She couldn't afford to have him for an enemy, but she'd rather lose everything than sleep with a man in exchange for anything.

When Ruby-Lynn, a new girl who'd just arrived from Chicago, neared, Mae touched her arm. The redhead smiled. "Yes Miss Mae?"

"Go to the man over there, the one with the red silk handkerchief in his pocket. Keep him company and ensure he's taken care of. No charge."

How she hated catering to the man, but her girls depended on her for their living, not to mention Miss Lady. Mae frowned at Ruby-Lynn's retreating back. She'd find a way to get Butch Mason to lose interest. An idea would come to her hopefully sooner than later.

"What's gotten into you Mae?" Miss Lady's concerned face was partly turned from her even though Mae could tell the older woman scowled. Sitting in her favorite place, a corner behind the piano, the older woman could watch the goings on and not be bothered by all the commotion, as she was prone to say. "You frownin' 'stead of smilin'."

Mae placed her hand on Miss Lady's thin shoulder and smiled down at her, careful to remove all signs of frustration. Ever since the slight woman came to look after her when she was a toddler, Miss Lady always seemed to sense every one of her emotions. After so many years Miss Lady was more a mother than caregiver or housekeeper. It had come that Mae could not see living without her.

"Nothing you have to worry about Miss Lady," she replied airily and bent to press a kiss on the soft mahogany cheek. "That damn Butch tried to get fresh with me in the back hallway, demanding and threatening as usual. I held him off and just now sent Molly-Lynn over to placate him."

"We need to just get Big James to kick his no-good carcass out," Miss Lady huffed, scanning the room in search of her new nemesis. "He'll think twice 'bout messin' with you. The man has no scruples."

The oversized bartender, James, looked over at hearing his name, and Mae shook her head to let him know all was well. If only she could do it, she'd have Mason thrown out a long time ago, but her hands were bound. "Now Miss Lady, don't you go fretting. You know I can take care of myself. Besides Captain McClain happened by, and Butch went on his way."

"Did he now?" Miss Lady cackled. "I bet the handsome Captain told him a thing or two about bothering you. He is a man of worth, sees after his own."

Mae took a breath and looked about the room to see if the new subject of their conversation had returned from out back. Perhaps the Captain had left after all. "No Miss Lady, he didn't say anything to Butch. Probably thought we were fooling around. You know John McClain always thinks the worse of me." Her chest constricted, and she forced the annoyance away. It did not matter what the man thought of her. Most people would agree with him.

"Well no matter what he thinks, a man should always come to the aid of a lady." Miss Lady huffed and patted her hand. "I think he sees you with different eyes, as what you are. And you is worthy Mae Hawkins."

"Look Miss Lady, that boy is dragging Janelle out to dance. He's about to get some sore feet. You know she can't dance a lick." Mae purposely changed the conversation and was grateful when Miss Lady began to chuckle and clap along with the music. Glad for the reprieve from Miss Lady's inferring that she should be treated like a lady, Mae moved away to circle about the room and greet customers.

One of her girls stuck her head from the hallway and scanned the room until locking on Mae. Pale and shaking, the girl beckoned, hands moving fast.

At seeing her pallid face, Mae hurried closer. "Are you all right? Calm down before you attract attention. Whatever is the matter with you?"

The girl's mouth opened, but only air exited, no with no sound coming. She held one hand to flat against her chest and pointed toward the kitchen with the other. "I think there's a dead man out back. He's laid out on the ground." She heaved a shaky breath. "I was about to go out to get fresh air and tripped over him."

Her heart quickened, and Mae released a gasp, but quickly recovered and forced a calm façade. "Goodness. I will fetch James. Now you go upstairs and splash cold water on your face. Stay there and get some rest. And don't say a word to anyone." The girl's head bobbed up and down and she flew from the entryway up the stairs.

Mae turned away and took her time walking through the saloon to not rouse too much attention. Once she reached the bar, she waited to get James' attention and whispered for the burly bartender to follow her. "Wait just a few moments. I don't want to attract unwarranted notice," she instructed the man gave a barely perceptive nod in return. Mae stopped to make small talk as she made her way out of the saloon, dreading what she'd find once she exited the house.

Who could it be? No one was missing.

The kitchen door remained open. The cool breeze blew through the airy space, but she barely noticed in her rush to see who the unfortunate person was. Mae picked up her skirts and stepped through the doorway.

At first she didn't seen anyone, then she looked straight

down and froze. A pale John McClain lay sprawled on the ground, eyes shut, not moving.

"Well I'll be damned, it's Captain McClain," James brushed past her, grunted when he leaned over the unconscious man running his hands over John's body. "You reckon someone shot him?" He peered closer at the man lying on the ground. "I don't see no blood. He's clean passed out or dead." The man pressed a finger to the side of John's throat. "I can't tell if there's a pulse."

Mae's heart stopped, and she reached out to the bannister to keep from collapsing. "Are you sure? Try again."

"Where have you two gotten to?" Miss Lady admonished from the kitchen. "The customers are thirsty, need James to man the bar." Miss lady walked out and stood next to her only to stiffen. "Oh goodness sakes, why isn't that Captain McClain?" Miss Lady pushed past a still nonmoving Mae and then shoved James away from John with surprising strength. "What are you doing James? Just looking at the man ain't helping none."

The gentle giant stood next to Miss Lady. "I don't see any injury, no blood." James straightened with his arms hanging to his sides and kept an eye on Miss Lady.

Miss Lady felt John's forehead and pressed her fingers onto the side of his neck. "He ain't dead. James pick 'em up and carry 'em inside to the bedroom just past the kitchen." Her sharp eyes met Mae's next. "For goodness sakes child, don't just stand there! Go open the bedroom door for James and get some cool water. The man is burning up with fever."

The stilled heart in her chest began to pound, and she felt

air entering her lungs. When James had pronounced John dead, the very ability to breathe left completely. Her world stopped, and an all-consuming darkness threatened to overcome. Surely John would be all right. They just had to nurse him and ensure he rested.

Mae forced her mind away from the thoughts and shifted into action when James moved past her to toward the house with John in his arms. With quick steps, Mae raced back up the porch steps. To assure herself more than anything, she reached and touched John's heated face. He was warm, actually quite hot.

After James went down the hallway, having to turn sideways to get his burden through, she rushed past him to hold the door open for him. Once the bartender made it through the doorway, she rushed to the kitchen, filled a pitcher with cool water and grabbed a pile of clean linens from a sideboard. It was imperative that she be there when John woke. She needed to witness his eyes opening.

It didn't make sense. John seemed fine earlier when she'd spoken to him. Yes, he'd seemed overheated, but she'd attributed his flushed coloring to riding out in the sun and the overheated room. He was ill. She caught up with Miss Lady who was about to enter the room.

James and Miss Lady made quick work of removing John's clothing. Once the shirt was removed and James had pulled his boots off, he hesitated looking up at Miss Lady. "I need to take his britches off."

Miss Lady nodded, "Yes, he's bleeding from his right leg. We need to see what he's got going on there." The tiny woman turned and pushed Mae out the door. "You wait outside. I'll call you back in once he's covered up."

"Oh for goodness sakes Miss Lady," Mae exclaimed. "I've seen a man without his pants on." In spite of her protests, she found herself outside the door as Miss Lady shoved her with force and slammed the door behind her. With a resigned sigh, Mae paced back and forth with ill concealed impatience. Who'd shot John and why? Did someone hide outside and wait to shoot him when he'd exited the house? Perhaps he'd been mistaken for someone else. She hesitated and strained to hear what was happening in the bedroom when several of the girls walked past her to the kitchen. They didn't notice her agitation, and she was thankful for it. For now they needed to keep what happened quiet.

"Come on in Mae," Miss Lady finally announced, cracking the door. Before she could enter the room, James rushed past her and went toward the saloon.

"Where is he going in such a hurry?" Mae asked and went to the bed to look down at the still unconscious John.

"I told him to find the most sober soldier, so I can send him to go fetch the doctor."

Mae rushed to the bedside and peered down at a shirtless, John had a wet cloth on his brow and blankets tucked neatly beneath his arms. His damp mahogany brown hair clung to the sides of his flushed handsome face. It was odd to see him so still, so vulnerable. Her eyes lingered on his enticing parted lips. "Is he going to be all right Miss Lady?"

"He's been shot, twice. Not today. Looks like days ago," Miss Lady stated, lifting the blanket to expose his right leg.

Mae's eyes widened at seeing the two angry wounds, one in his upper thigh and the second on his calf. Both leaked a yellowish liquid entwined with red blood.

"He's in a bad way. The wounds are infected," Miss Lady answered her silent question.

Mae pressed her palm against her chest. "Why was he here instead of somewhere recovering? He must have been in a lot of pain." A shiver traveled up her spine, and she trembled. "He should have remained at the post. In bed…"

Without opening his eyes, John moaned and winced when Miss Lady began to poke at the wounds. "I'm going to boil some water and clean it out. When I get back, I may need you to hold him still. Remain here, hold him down if he begins to stir too much, sooth him. Talk to him, keep him calm." Miss Lady instructed. "Sing if you have to. He may hear you, and it will help settle him."

"Sing?" Mae lifted an eyebrow. "That would probably push him closer to death."

A soldier burst into the room, his uniform askew and hat in hand. He stopped just inside the doorway, eyes darted to each of them before snapping first to his captain before focusing on the injured leg. The young man turned a light shade of green, yet he maintained a strong unwavering voice. "W-What happened to the Captain?" Without moving from the doorway, he looked to Miss Lady as if she held the answer to all his questions.

The slight woman guided him out to the hallway, and he didn't fight her. "I need you to go into town. Looks like the Captain was shot days ago, and it's infected. Tell the doc to come out here, and make sure you tell him it's for Captain McClain. He may not hurry if he thinks it's one of our girls ailing." The hallway became silent as both the soldier and Miss Lady left to complete the tasks at hand.

John moaned but did not open his eyes, still unconscious, and Mae took the now heated cloth from his brow plunging it back into the cool water. She placed it back on his brow and took his hand in hers. "John can you hear me? You'll be all right, don't fret, please just try to rest." His brow crinkled and she smiled. "I'll take that frown as a sign you can hear me. You don't like me to call you by your first name for some reason. Sometimes I wonder why that is. Never considered asking you. Perhaps once you wake up, I will. I will ask you John."

With a loud groan, he arched from the bed, his back bowing high above the mattress. Mae swallowed hard not liking how much pain he was in while caressing his clenched jaw. "Oh God, I'm so sorry, I wish there was something I could do. "Shhh, shhh," she whispered in his ear while continuing to stroke his face. She repeated the shushing noises until, finally, he lowered back to the bed and seemed to calm. Either that or he passed out from the pain.

Moments later, the door opened and Miss Lady bustled in with a container of hot water. The woman bent to place the pot on the floor next to the bed, her worried eyes on the unconscious man.

Mae brushed the back of her free hand across the tops of her cheeks, surprised to find them wet.

Miss Lady missed nothing. "What's the matter honey?"

"I—I feel so bad to see him in so much pain. I think he

passed out."

She was grateful when Miss Lady did not make an issue of her tears. "Well it's a good thing he's out right now. I can get the wound cleaned out good without him feeling too much of it then. Just in case, be ready to hold him down." After a firm nod to ensure Mae understood, Miss Lady began to dip cloths into the hot water and cleaned the wound.

A LITTLE OVER an hour later, even with the kitchen door open that allowed for the breeze to blow in, Mae fanned her overheated face while pacing around the sizeable kitchen table.

One of the two soldiers who'd fallen asleep slumped over the table, snored and adjusted his head on folded arms.

Mae moved away from the table and closer to Miss Lady so not to wake them and whispered. "I don't understand why we can't remain in the room while the doctor examines him." She picked up her glass of water and drank it all down before replacing it. "What if the doctor has questions, needs someone to hand him items? Or what if John takes a turn for the worse? Shouldn't we be in there to help?" Mae placed her hands on her hips and looked down at the older woman who sat in a chair with a serene expression, looking out the doorway into the darkness. "Honestly, I don't understand how you can be so calm right now Miss Lady?"

The chair creaked as Miss Lady stood and took one of Mae's hands then led her to the doorway. They stood side by side in the narrow entry. Mae not sure what Miss Lady intended, waited without a word. "Look up there," Miss Lady instructed pointing at the sky. "Do you see all 'em stars?"

Still unsure of where Miss Lady was going with this, Mae looked up to the sky and nodded. "Yes Miss Lady, it's a starry night."

"Well you see, God knows each one of 'em, made them and placed them. And now us being his children, well he knows each of us even more. Right now, he is watching over the captain. There ain't nothin' any of us can do for him that the Lord isn't already takin' care of. Frettin' surely won't help, but prayin' and askin' for his help does. That's what I've been doin'."

Eyes cast downward, Mae leaned against the slight woman. "You're right Miss Lady. I don't know why I'm acting up like this. You've taught me better. It's just that seeing him so weak, it's so dreadful. He's always been such a strong healthy man."

"Still is," Miss Lady smiled up at her. "Its why he will be all right." Her eyes twinkled. "'Sides, I know the real reason you're frettin' so is because you're sweet on him. I understand that. Captain McClain is a very handsome man, and you can't help yourself." She chuckled at Mae's gasp. "Honey it shows every time he comes around. Your face lights up."

"Oh!" Mae's mouth fell open. "You are mistaken, I am not 'sweet' on him or anybody." She drew away and went back to the kitchen just as two of the working girls walked in, both giggling loudly. They went to sit down when Miss Lady shook her head at them. "Oh no you don't. Both of you are in serious need of fresh air. Looks like you've been taking a drink or two of the hard stuff." Both of the women's eyes widened and flew to Mae before they attempted to hurry through the kitchen.

Mae stuck her arm out and blocked the now subdued women as they tried to hurry past her. "Stop right there." They froze and faced her.

She glared at each of the girls for a moment. "You cannot provide good services to the gentlemen if you are drunk, therefore they will not pay. If they don't pay, we don't eat. Simple. As. That. If you dare take but another sip of alcohol, you will pack your things and go." She met each of their now scared stares for a beat. "Am I understood?" Both girls nodded, heads bobbing with alarming speed. "Now go and get fresh air for a few minutes and then come back in here and drink some strong coffee." Mae slid her eyes to the soldiers who somehow managed to sleep through it all. Funny what exhaustion did to a person.

Just as the girls hustled outside, the doctor walked in and stood just inside the kitchen entryway.

Mae studied his face hoping she could read by his expressions how John fared. Miss Lady roused the closest soldier, who rubbed his face and straightened immediately upon seeing the doctor. He then shook the other soldier awake.

Miss Lady regarded the physician. "Well Doc, how is Captain McClain? Can he be taken back to his post? These soldiers are waitin' to hear."

Doctor Martin pressed his lips together and reached out to accept a cup of coffee Mae poured for him. His kind eyes met hers for a beat. Even though his temples had wisps of gray, the doctor was not an old man. While he only stepped into the brothel if one of the working girls was sick, he'd always treated them with respect and kindness. "Captain McClain is very sick" The doctor began and then regarded the men in the room. "You can go on back to the post and let your commander know he should not be moved right now." He regarded Mae next. "In my opinion, the Captain can't be moved for a while yet, at least a couple of weeks." He wrote a note and gave it to one of the soldiers. "Give that to the doc, and he can decide what he wants to do."

The man sipped his coffee as Miss Lady fussed with the soldiers, walking them outside.

"Miss Mae, how are you tonight?" Doctor Martin asked giving her a quizzical look. "Are you unwell?"

"I'm fine thank you. Just tired. Is Jo—Captain McClain's life in danger?" Her voice trembled at the last word, and she lifted her chin, attempting a look of indifference.

"Well I gave him some drops for the pain. Miss Lady did a good job of cleaning the wounds. He came to long enough to disagree with what I told him may have to be done if the infection continues to get worse. So to answer your question Miss Mae, his life is in danger if the infection in his wounds keeps progressing. All you can do for now is keep it clean and dry." The doctor yawned and put the cup down. He placed his hat on his head and picked up the worn medical bag he'd dropped beside him. "Continue with the cool compresses and cleanings. I will be back in a couple of days. If he gets worse, send someone to fetch me."

Silver dollars sparkled in the light when Mae held them out to the doctor who accepted the payment and left. The infection would not get worse, and John would recover fully. She'd see to for herself. With a cup of coffee in hand, Mae hustled down the hall to check on the patient.

A soft snore sounded within the dim room. John didn't rouse when she entered and closed the door behind. Whatever Doctor Martin had given him ensured he slept soundly it seemed. She neared the bed and felt his brow. Although still warm, he'd cooled down considerably. After dipping the cloth back into the cold water, she wiped his face and then placed a fresh compress on his brow. Somewhat assured, Mae set about straightening the blankets. She lifted the blanket to see the doctor had re-bandaged the leg. What had the doctor meant about John disagreeing with 'what had to be done'?

"MAE?" THE HUSKY male voice woke her, and she blinked and jerked to look toward the bed. Barely opened dark gray eyes studied her. "Where am I?"

"Still here at my house," Mae ran the back of her hand up her cheek and yawned. "You passed out in the back yard…" It was then she noticed his eyes were glazed and moving constantly from one end of the room to the other. "John, how do you feel?" He didn't need to answer her question. By the sheen of perspiration on his brow and the flush of his face, the fever had returned.

John attempted to sit up, but gave up. "Is that a dog?"

"Dog?" She followed the path of his vision; he stared at the floor near the door. "What dog John?"

A soft moan sounded, and John closed his eyes. His lips moved yet he could not form any words. When she placed a fresh cool rag on his, his eyes jerked open and locked onto her face. "You're beautiful Maebelle. I've always admired your loveliness." The upward curve of his lips made her heart skip. "You can never know how hard it is to not touch you."

"Whatever are you talking about?"

His eyes closed, so he'd fallen asleep again. Mae remained frozen long listening to John's even breathing. How true were his words? All nonsense. Especially after seeing a dog. Of course, he must have mistaken her for someone else. The words from a feverish man meant nothing.

It was evening now, and the sounds of laughter followed by a new livelier song made her wonder if perhaps, once the medication wore off, the captain would not be able to get enough rest. She frowned toward the doorway. Nothing could be done about it. This was a house where the nights were filled with activity and the days quieted while everyone slept.

To allow some of the stuffiness out of the room, Mae opened the window. She leaned into the welcome cool breeze.

A man and one of her girls passed outside the window, speaking and laughing. She shook her head and let out a resigned sigh. "It's going to be hard to ensure you get enough rest around here at night John."

John grumbled in his sleep, seeming to agree with her, and she smiled toward the bed. Either her voice or the sound of his name when she said it brought out a reaction almost every time.

Chapter Three

LIKE CLAWS PEELING his flesh away, pain seared up his leg. John gritted his teeth and stretched it, forcing the stiff limb to become accustomed to movement. Back and forth, he flexed first from the knee down and then from the hip, each movement becoming easier, smoother.

For two weeks, he'd been holed up in the house, in the same room. Each time he attempted to venture out, either Miss Lady or Mae would catch him and shoo him back into the room and to bed. Too weak from the blinding pain shooting through his leg when he stood to resist and since the dizziness came when he tried to stand upright, he'd not had much choice but to comply.

Today was a rare break. Upon awakening, the first thing he'd noticed was that the pain had lessoned considerably. Now after completing the exercises prescribed by Doctor Martin, he was in pain, but not unbearable.

Sitting on a chair near the window, he'd spotted Miss Lady and Mae outside. They walked towards the road, and he made up his mind to seize the opportunity to move around, get out of the cramped room.

His soldiers hadn't returned since they'd come two days

earlier. He wasn't sure any of his regiment would anymore, not to see him anyway. During the last visit, they'd delivered his discharge papers, pay and belongings. Before leaving, they'd shook his hand and wished him well. One of the soldiers who'd been under his command shuffled his feet while the young man informed him the unit was about to be disbanded. Those who wished to continue in the military would be relocated to other posts.

He eyed the small pile of items in the corner of the room. *Time to move on McClain.* He tested his weight on his healthy leg and pushed up from the chair with his arms to stand. The swaying of the room was only slight, which was comforting. With measured movements, he lowered his left leg until his foot rested flat on the floor.

One step. The pain was bearable. He shifted and took a second step.

It was slow progress, with the short distance from his room to the front room taking him much longer than he had expected. Without the evening crowds, the space seemed much bigger. He went to the large polished mahogany bar and leaned forward to study the lines of neatly lined clean glasses along the back wall. It smelled of tobacco and drink, yet it was a pleasant space.

When John finally approached the bedroom, he heard female voices. Mae and Miss Lady had returned and were in the kitchen.

The tone of Mae's voice caught his attention, so instead of returning to the room, John leaned against the wall and listened.

"Miss Lady, why did you read the letter? I told you over and again I want nothing to do with the man." Although the words were spoken rapidly, Mae maintained her tone soft.

Miss Lady huffed, and he could hear the older woman shuffling across the floor. "You're right Mae. He don't deserve a thing from you. You on the other hand, deserve much from him. You need to go west to Texas and see what your daddy has to offer. His letter says he wants to leave you his property. A large ranch. If nothing else, you can sell the ranch and come back with enough money to move away from here, start a new life. Maybe you can go north."

"Where exactly would I go?" Mae's voice cracked, and John wondered if she was crying. "I can't go far enough in this state to escape someone knowing about my life here. Somewhere someone will recognize me. You know well and good my mother's family up north has made it abundantly clear I'm not welcome. I know you mean well Miss Lady, but please just let it go."

"This is one thing I am not going to let go Mae." Miss Lady's tone was harsh. "You can be mad all you want, but I'm puttin' you on a stagecoach west if it's the last thing I do." Her next statement startled John. "Captain McClain, what are you doing out of bed?"

Before he could take a step, both women rushed over and flanked him. Hands pushed up on his elbows urged him toward a chair in the kitchen.

Mae kept her face turned away, as if hiding evidence of distress. Yet her words were clear, strong. "Of all the stubborn things John McClain, why didn't you call? One of us can bring you anything you need. Doctor Martin doesn't want you up until he returns and pronounces you well enough to be up and about. After his last visit, he said your leg is still too injured, slow to heal."

"I can't abide staying in the room another day," John told them feeling childish when both women stood over him with balled hands on their hips. "I have to get moving so I can be on my way soon. Can't continue to abuse your hospitality and good care," he finished looking up at them with a scowl.

The words seemed to placate them both, Miss Lady moved toward the stove. "Well, I can certainly understand how hard it's been for you to be shut inside the room all these days. Unfortunately you need the recovery time lest you fall sick again. Let me pour you some coffee Captain."

Mae brushed past him, her soft floral fragrance a familiar scent now. "I'll go see about freshening your linens and getting the room aired out." She turned to look at Miss Lady. "I'll be in my room for a spell afterwards."

"Our conversation is not over young lady," Miss Lady called after the retreating form. The older woman turned her attention to John. "I never thought I'd meet anyone more mule-headed person than my Mae, until you Captain McClain. Now what is your hurry to leave all about?"

John accepted the coffee and looked over the top of his cup out the window. "My plans are to go out west Miss Lady." He wondered how much to tell. "I've got someone to look for in Texas. And the sooner I catch up to 'em, the better."

She frowned, and nodded in understanding. "You're welcome to stay as long as you need Captain McClain. It's best not to hurry healin'. I know you have plans and such, but it ain't gonna do you any good to hurry to leave only to end up back in a sick bed."

There was no arguing the point. "I do need to check on my horse. He's rather unruly, and it's hard for a stranger to tend to him."

"You ain't goin' out there to the stables no time soon. Not until Doc says you can. James has a way with animals, and your mount's been doing well enough." Miss Lady's tone left little room for argument. "'Sides, I doubt you can make it halfway to the barn in your condition, much less makin' to go nowhere. Give it another few days Captain McClain. Whatever it is that needs to be done can wait."

Miss Lady was right of course. Instead of a response, John sighed and stared out the window toward the barn.

THREE DAYS LATER, John woke to the usually quite morning at the brothel. Everyone slept late in the place, and he was thankful for the respite from the laughter, music and smoke. He rolled to his back and stretched. Other than a slight tightness in his leg, there was no pain now. Glad for the reprieve from the aching, he lay in bed a few minutes longer enjoying the first morning without pain.

Doctor Martin had grudgingly agreed he could venture out for short walks. The outdoors beckoned, and John got up. He took his time washing up and dressing, not wanting to push it and do any damage to the healing injury.

Making his way toward the kitchen he hoped to avoid

running into anyone. Not a morning person, he preferred solitude upon waking. Thankfully the room was empty.

When he exited to the back porch, John inhaled the fresh air and stretched; it felt good to be outside. The crisp air filled his lungs lifting his spirits, and his gaze followed a flock of birds flying in a precise formation across the pale blue sky. It was definitely a good way to begin the day. He would give it just another couple days and then leave, with or without Doctor Martin's approval. It was time.

Although his leg was still newly healed, he couldn't afford to wait much longer to get on the road west to find the outlaw. If the man remained in Texas, he'd seek out the damned woman who was with him and get answers to the questions he'd planned to ask the day he'd been shot.

John crossed the wide expanse from the house to the stables, his steps slow yet steady.

The inside of the barn was dim when John entered it, looking to find his horse. The clean stables and pens along with the smell of fresh hay relieved some of the guilt over the animal being penned for so long. Like him, the animal preferred the outdoors. Fresh air, lack of walls and confinement were their lifeblood.

Four stalls later, he still hadn't found the horse. Had the soldiers taken him? No, it was not possible. He'd paid for the horse, ensured they'd signed the papers turning the animal over to him. The unruly beast would buck off and trample to death anyone who tried to ride him other than John.

Alarmed now, he hurried out the back of the barn and held his hand over his eyes prepared to look to the horizon for a sign of the horse. Only a few feet from the back door, under the shade of an overhang, his beast pranced and preened while a blonde in plain brown skirts and a sturdy blouse brushed his mane. "There you go handsome sir. I appreciate you allowing me to ride you." The woman's hand caressed the content horse's nose. "Now how about you spend some time in the corral, since you seem to dislike the barn so much?"

"Mae?" John could have bitten his tongue off for speaking out loud when she jumped and dropped the brush.

The beauty turned to face him and lifted a brow, perfecting the look of total annoyance. "If Miss Lady finds you out here, she'll not be too happy."

"I'm well enough that I can come see about my horse," John replied eyeing the animal nuzzling Mae's hand. The traitor of a horse no doubt had fallen under the spell of a striking female. Mae pushed him away. "Not now horse."

"His name is Lasitor."

Mae turned to his horse and grabbed the reins, pulling it toward the corral. "Come horse, you can get a tasty carrot once you do as you're told, unlike your owner who won't listen to a thing, even if it's good for him." Lasitor turned and eyed him as if agreeing with Mae and walked docile as a lamb, beside her.

John followed the pair not sure what to do. If she were one of his men, he'd be hollering and demand she release the reins. Why didn't he do it now? Well she was a female, yet she was purposely taking the horse away.

"I demand you drop those reins this instant woman and allow me some time with my horse. Shouldn't you be asleep or taking care of whatever things you do in the house?" No sooner did the harsh words leave his mouth than he knew he was about to see a side of the Madam he'd yet to imagine.

Her skirts swirled around her ankles when she spun. Sparks brightened the green eyes tunneled into his, and her top lip twisted into a snarl. She practically threw the reins at Lasitor, who blinked when the leather flew across his muzzle. The horse obviously the smarter of the two males moved a few feet away into the corral and began to nibble on the grass.

John remained planted, prepared for a hearty slap if not worse as he watched Mae stomp closer.

"Now listen here Captain McClain. I don't expect much from you. I certainly don't want your gratitude or any type of compensation for keeping your sorry hide here. Unlike the horse, you have been nothing but an irritable, infuriating mule the entire time. I am nobody's woman. Don't you ever demand anything from me!"

She blinked her eyes were shiny with angry tears. "Now if you would excuse me, I have better things to do than to waste my time and energy on the likes of you." With one last glare she went toward the house.

Head hanging down, he could hear the bustling of her skirts become fainter.

"I am nobody's woman." Her words sunk in. She looked on the verge of crying. Damn it, he would have preferred the slap.

Chapter Four

BY THE TIME Mae made it inside the kitchen, she shook so hard, her teeth rattled. Never had she met a more infuriating person than John McClain. How could he stand there and order her about? Demand things? As if she were one of his men no less. His tone of superiority, the way he'd eluded to her work tore her in half. She had no illusions that anyone would ever treat her with respect. Even so, there was such a thing as human kindness wasn't there? With an angry swipe, she slid the back of her hand across her wet cheeks. The angry tears made her even angrier. She shouldn't let him affect her this way. Besides, she should be used to being treated in such a manner.

At the sound of footsteps coming from the back porch, she gathered up her skirts to flee, only to the damn folds become tangled with a chair so that she was yanked backward. Tugging free, she ignored the tall shadow spilling over the room. "Miss Mae," John McClain cleared his throat. "Can I speak to you for a moment?"

Since when did he call her 'Miss'? Mae stopped with her back to him. "No I don't have time with things needing to be done here in the house. I have much to do Captain McClain.

You can speak to Miss Lady about anything you require when she returns in a bit from her walk." She went toward the hallway.

"I apologize for speaking to you in the manner of which I did." The huskiness in his voice told he was not used to apologizing for anything. "I was out of line."

Mae turned to face him and knew immediately it was a mistake when his concerned gray eyes pinned her. The sincerity in them shocked her, the depth of his gaze holding her prisoner. "Miss Mae, I am not ungrateful for what you and Miss Lady have done for me. I do understand both of you have done a great deal to help in my recovery. If I gave the impression of a foul mood," he paused when she arched a brow. "What I mean to say is that I was unhappy at being indoors for so long. I am not of a good temper in the mornings, but there is no excuse for my behavior. I should have minded my temper better. And I do plan to repay you for everything. I've never seen Lasitor so well behaved. He's been well taken care of, both of us have. Please accept my apology." Eyes locked on hers, he waited for an answer and she found it impossible to look away, her heartbeat quickened and her mouth became dry at his close scrutiny.

He cleared his throat and it broke the spell.

"Just let me be." Mae waved him off, angered at her feeble and lackluster sound of her words.

"What is going on here?" Miss Lady came up behind John, and Mae fought the urge to flee. She wouldn't give John the satisfaction of knowing how much he affected her.

Mae motioned to John. "Captain McClain was just apologizing for being a horse's ass."

"Mae Hawkins," Miss Lady admonished. "Mind your language." Miss Lady turned to the Captain. "I overheard some of it. From the sounds of it, you did right to apologize to Mae. She is to be treated with respect due a lady at all times and especially in this house." Properly chastised, John studied his boots.

"Miss Lady," Mae protested only to hush when Miss Lady pinned her with an arched brow.

John cleared his throat. "I do owe both you and Miss Mae an apology. I have not been a gentleman, and I apologize."

"I accept your apology," Miss Lady told him and then turned to Mae. "And you child?"

Mae raised flat eyes to him. "I'm not sure," she grumbled.

Miss Lady looked to be somewhat mollified, and then she turned to John. "As I said, I overheard part of what you said, especially the part of you repaying us. It so happens I have an idea for the amount of repayment." Her eyes slid to Mae, and she knew in that instant Miss Lady was about to rope her into something she could not get out of.

John looked between them with narrowed eyes, but he remained silent.

Lips curving into a mischievous grin, Miss Lady took time to smooth her skirts and then wagged a finger at Mae. "You should accept his apology Mae."

Her throat dry, Mae cleared it and nodded, looking past the glowering captain's left shoulder. "I accept your apology John. As far as payment, there is no..."

"No need to repay us with money," Miss Lady interrupted.

"As I recall, you have plans to go west to take care of some situation or another. It would keep this old woman's mind at ease if you would agree to accompany Mae, as she has to go to see about things in Texas too."

Old woman? Miss Lady sure knew how to wind a person around her little finger, and Mae could see John faltering to come up with a way out of having to escort her. Mae smirked at him from behind Miss Lady, goading him to come up with a good excuse to be away from the 'likes' of her. For a brief moment, he appeared to be at a loss for words.

When John locked stares with her, Mae felt the first trickle of dread. Eyes twinkling, he slid his gaze away from her. *Challenge accepted.* "Miss Lady, it would be my pleasure to escort Miss Mae anywhere she needs to go." His eyes gleamed with amusement when they met her widened ones. "I'll deliver her safe and sound exactly where you tell me. I assure you she will be protected. You should not be worried about such a thing."

No! This is not what was supposed to happen.

"What dear?" Miss Lady's innocent expression turned to her. She'd spoken out loud. "Did you say no? Surely you understand this is the answer to my prayers. I've been praying to God to help find a way for you to safely go see about your father."

"The stagecoach is safe enough," Mae gritted out. "Besides I am not prepared to travel as soon as I'm sure the Captain plans to leave. Didn't you tell me he plans to leave in a day or two?" She gave the smug man a pointed glare. "Besides, we don't have a covered wagon, and I cannot ride astride for days at a time. It's impossible. Thank you for your offer of assistance Captain McClain. I will go see about a stagecoach ticket in a day or two."

The hateful man cocked his head to the side. "You make a valid point Miss Mae. Riding astride for such a long journey could prove tiring with my injured leg. Come to think of it, I need to take all my belongings as well, so I need a good-sized wagon. Heck, I've plenty of money saved, so I will purchase a small covered wagon. It could come in handy, as I will need a place to sleep and live out of once I arrive in Texas. It will be at least a couple of days by the time I get everything settled. Plenty of time to pack, wouldn't you say Miss Lady?"

Miss Lady nodded, her eyes pinning Mae with a "don't say another word look". "Yes Captain, I do believe it's just enough time to get Mae more than ready to travel."

This could not be happening. Mae flew from the room straight up to hers. "*No!*"

Chapter Five

Two days later

WHAT THE HELL had he done? John paced back in forth in the now familiar guest bedroom. No sooner did he finish his breakfast than he'd returned to the room. All morning he'd remained secluded, needing some privacy before preparing for the long days on the trail. Sitting on the bed, he closed his eyes and ran his fingers through the thick, overgrown hair now past his neckline. Absently he considered that it had never before been this length.

He looked up to the ceiling. "Lord help me, but I'm in trouble."

The thought of weeks on the trail alone with a beautiful woman was not the only reason he paced. What would she dress like? If she dressed like she did every night, although not as scandalous compared to other women in the brothel, her manner of dress would not work well for travel. Would he have to put up with her attempting to earn money the only way she knew how along the way? He should have asked Miss Lady for some ground rules before giving his word to escort Mae to Texas.

Heck, anyone with half a brain would have backed out of

the agreement. He couldn't be blamed by anyone if he did. What was more important in this instance, though, was that he was a man of his word and Miss Lady trusted him, her intelligent eyes seeming to know more about him than even he hoped to. Her gentle and caring ways toward Mae made him wonder why the woman was so watchful over the Madam. From what he gathered, Mae's mother left Miss Lady to raise her. He wasn't sure if Mae's mother had died or just left. He admired Miss Lady. It seemed the poor older woman considered the prostitute like a daughter.

Well, no time to rethink things. He'd just make the best of the situation. Mae would just have to abide by his stipulations. He'd wait until they were on the road and then explain things to her. Surely she'd not be so stubborn as to disagree. And if she did, well she'd just have to find herself a new way to get to Texas. He slammed his fist into the bedding. No, he couldn't do it. There was no way would that he abandon her along the road. He'd given Miss Lady his word.

"Captain McClain?" The bartender James' deep voice called from the other side of the closed door. "I'm about to load Miss Hawkins' things. Do you want to oversee where we put 'em?"

Oh yes, he'd oversee this. Mae had barely left her room the last two days. She would not be allowed to take more than a couple trunks, so whatever mountain she'd been packing would be left behind. "I'm coming," he replied, picking up his hat and heading toward the doorway. He took one last look around his living space of the last three weeks. The room, although simple, had been comfortable. Yet, if he never saw the inside of a brothel again, he wouldn't be bothered by it in the least.

The sun shone through the filter of the light clouds. John donned his hat and looked around. Other than a woman in dark dress and Miss Lady, the only person in sight was James, puffing as he dragged a bag of feed across to the wagon. John walked over and helped the man lift the bag onto back of the carriage. He peered inside to see only one additional trunk added to the items he'd already loaded. He looked to Miss Lady. "Where are the rest of her belongings? I know she packed more than this."

"I have the small truck and this one bag here, that's all."

He jerked to look at the woman standing next to Miss Lady. Wearing a dark serviceable dress with a matching hat, Mae's eyes met his from under the brim. She held a carpetbag in one hand and had a heavy cape draped over her arm. Her eyes narrowed at his risen eyebrows. "Well, Captain McClain, it seems you have a lot of preconceived notions about me."

Definitely an understatement.

"Captain McClain?" A masculine voice called.

When a young male appeared from the side of the house, John looked at the assembled group, but no one seemed to be expecting him. Jefferson, a Calvary soldier, although not one of his, removed his worn hat and nodded at the women upon approaching. "I was told you was headed west, and I'd be obliged if you'd allow me to tag along." Jefferson extended a fistful of money toward John. "I'm willing to pay and help with the driving so you can rest."

This development was the answer to his prayers. John waved the money away. "You'll have to ride in the back."

Jefferson's eyes slid toward Mae and widened slightly. Other than that, he kept his composure and nodded in agreement. "Yes sir, thank you sir." He ran back and returned with a small bundle, which he threw into the wagon before climbing in.

After Mae and Miss Lady embraced and said tearful goodbyes, John assisted Mae to the front seat of the wagon. She sat with her face devoid of expression and looked straight ahead, not looking at anyone. He went to go around the wagon to climb up when Miss Lady placed a hand on his arm staying him. She pulled him away from the group, and she raised her tear-filled eyes to him. "Now Captain, my girl is very precious to me. You gave me your word you'd look after her, and I trust you will." He started to speak, except she continued. "Now, I know she can be prideful and stubborn, but there is a lot about Mae you don't know. She's not as tough as she puts on so please don't be too harsh with her."

"No harm will come to Mae while she's with me. I will keep my word to you Miss Lady. Don't you worry. She'll be back here with you before you know it." He leaned and gave her soft brown cheek a kiss. "You keep yourself well Miss Lady."

Her lips curved into a soft smile. "I will. You take care of your leg young man."

After he climbed onto the bench next to Mae, he looked to her and pulled a blanket from under the seat. He rolled it and pushed it behind her back. "If you're going to sit so stiff like, you'll need some support for your back."

She huffed and refused to look to him. "Let's go please. The sooner I get there, the faster I can come home." The words were laced with something he couldn't quite discern. Could it be fear? Certainly the unflappable Mae Hawkins was not scared.

With a snap of the reins, he coaxed the horses onto the road. It surprised John that Lasitor seemed to not mind being harnessed to pull the wagon beside Mae's large farm horse. Soon they easily moved at a steady pace.

THE DAY WENT by without incident John, who preferred silence didn't mind the lack of conversation between himself and his companion. Mae's head bobbed a few times as sleep threatened, but each time she bolted back to her stiff straight position. John ignored her, knowing sooner or later she would be too exhausted to maintain the posture. He pulled a long drink from his canteen and offered it to her only to be annoyed when she shook her head.

"I have my own water, thank you," she told him motioning to a basket under her seat. "Miss Lady packed plenty of provisions for both of us. Although, now we have another one along, it may not go as far." Mae glanced over her shoulder. "Do you know him?"

John nodded. He knew about Jefferson, who'd been kicked out of the Calvary for misconduct. The boy had a nasty temper, and after the initial relief of having a third person along, John had been second-guessing his hasty decision. "Yes I know of him. He was not one of my men. He's been discharged from the regiment."

The answer seemed to satisfy her. She studied him for a

moment, and he wondered if she was about to ask another question. When he turned to face her, Mae looked forward again. It would be several hours before they would stop again since they'd taken a break not too long before, so he decided it was time to broach the subject of her behavior while on the road together.

He cleared his throat. "Mae, there is something we should discuss." Sharp eyes snapped to him for an instant before she promptly dropped them to her hands fingers entwined on her lap she listened. Why did he feel like a tongue-tied boy around this woman? For years he'd commanded hardened men, for Gods' sake. He swallowed and continued. "You see, what we need to get straight is although I don't agree with your lifestyle, I don't judge you either." If possible she sat up straighter and paled, and she did not speak. "However, during this trip I expect you will refrain from…"

"Stop the wagon at once!" Her hand flew to cover her mouth, and she leaned away over the side. For a minute he wasn't sure if she was about to become sick or jump from the wagon.

John pulled the horses to an abrupt stop, and Mae jumped to the ground. With her skirts pulled up, she dashed toward the tree line and out of sight. With no idea what happened, he decided to go after her in case she was ill. John looked to Jefferson who poked his head from the back of the wagon. "See about the horses. I'll be right back." The younger man climbed down and walked toward the horses.

He rushed toward the tree line only to see Mae returning. Her countenance composed, she straightened her hat and went to walk around him. "Are you unwell?"

Her flat eyes seemed to look through him. "I will ride in the back of the wagon. I need to sleep. Please tell Jefferson to ride up front." She pressed her lips together into a tight line. "And as for my behavior Captain McClain, I will endeavor to keep my skirt down and my legs together the entire time so as to not wound your sensibilities." She marched away from him and waited at the back of the wagon until he instructed the Jefferson to move any items he needed to the front.

Jefferson, who was more than happy to get out from the uncomfortable and bumpy wagon rear, smiled and hurriedly grabbed a small bundle from the rear before climbing onto the bench.

Mae ignored his outstretched hand and climbed into the back of the wagon. The basket Miss Lady had packed caught John's attention, so he grabbed it and took it to the back of the wagon. When he lifted the flap, Mae sat with her back pressed to the bag of feed, her hat removed and head bent. If he didn't know any better, he'd think she was praying. Without a word, he placed the basket into the wagon and left. He'd try to be careful, but regardless, she was in for a bumpy and uncomfortable ride.

The rest of the day progressed without incident. His thoughts constantly went to Mae, and he wondered if he'd misspoken. Her reaction took him by surprise. He'd expected the anger, but the initial reaction was strange. She'd acted hurt, broken, insulted. It was too late now; he couldn't take the words back.

THREE DAYS LATER, the setting sun gave plenty of light for an exhausted John to guide the horses to a clearing next to a stream. He and Jefferson unhitched the horses to allow them to feed and drink before placing blankets on their backs and tying them to low branches for the night.

Looking as tired as he felt, Mae climbed from the back of the wagon and, without a word, walked toward the nearby water.

Over the last three days, Jefferson had become bolder in his attention to Mae. Although she remained cool toward both of them, the male did not seem to be easily dissuaded. Twice John had warned him to keep his distance. Jefferson had only shrugged in response. Even now the young man's gaze followed her retreating figure with rapt interest. John hoped he'd not invited trouble when allowing the volatile man along. "Let's get some kindling for fire," John got his attention. "Then we'll unload our bedrolls. I figure Miss Mae will want to sleep in back of the wagon as usual, for privacy." The young man raised his eyebrows at his comment and nodded before heading toward the stream in the direction Mae went.

Through the trees, John spied them. They exchanged a few words, and Mae moved away, into the trees. She appeared a few moments later and returned to the back of the wagon.

Hours later, the flames danced casting shadows upon the ground. Jefferson lay on his bedroll, seeming to be asleep. John made one last trek to the stream to wash up and then headed to the wagon. "Mae, may I speak with you?" he called without lifting the flap. "Are you awake?"

She pulled the flap up and peered out at him. "What is it

Captain?"

"You don't have to remain back in the wagon the entire time we are stopped. Err… if you wish to sleep by the fire, it may be warmer. I can assist you with a bedroll."

Her eyes shifted toward the fire and lingered as if she were tempted. "That won't be necessary. I'm perfectly warm in here."

"Very well," he said moving back to where he'd sleep. "Good night."

"Good night," she replied, her voice soft.

"JOHN!" MUFFLED SOUNDS woke John. The unmistakable noise of a female in distress jerked him to sit up and scan the area around him. Jefferson was gone. He looked toward the wagon and Mae when a moan cut through the air.

Mae was in trouble.

He jumped to his feet and had taken a few steps toward the wagon when the second noise stopped him. This one was a deeper masculine tone. The groan followed by silence explained enough, so he needed no further explanation as to what occurred. John went back to his bedroll and sunk into it. John let out a breath. No matter how much he fought it, his gaze slid to the wagon. A weight crushed his chest making it hard to keep from growling in anger.

A shuffling noise sounded, and Jefferson hustled down from the wagon and hurried to the stream, not noticing that John watched him.

How could she do this? Did she need the money? No, she

did it as an affront. To prove to him he could not order her about. This entire journey was a monumental mistake, one he'd have to endure until the end. He'd keep his word to Miss Lady. Once they arrived in Texas, he'd never see or hear from Mae again, which suited him perfectly.

Moments later, Jefferson crawled into his bedroll while John pretended to sleep.

THE FACT JOHN felt rested the next morning surprised him since it had been a long while before he'd calmed enough to fall back to sleep. Jefferson was up and keeping busy looking after the horses and afterwards pacing by the stream.

Mae did not come for coffee as she'd made of habit of, and John did not go to her and offer. Finally she emerged from the wagon and went in the opposite direction of where Jefferson was to the stream.

Not able to help himself, John went after her. With graceful steps, Mae bent over the water's edge, presenting a pretty picture. Her head bowed, she pulled her hair back and knotted it at her nape, and then she kneeled to cup water with her hands and held the cool liquid up to her face. She repeated the motion several times.

When John approached, she straightened and shifted away from him. Her hair cascaded past her shoulders, freed from the pins, and Mae had her face turned away.

When he took her by the forearm, she flinched as if his touch burned. That a woman such as her could seem so fragile at times was disconcerting.

"I know what happened last night." He managed to keep his rage controlled, only by a thin hair. "I won't stand for what happened to repeat itself. I thought I made myself clear."

She trembled. Probably from the cold water, maybe she was upset, whatever it was he'd not let the reaction stop him from getting his point across. Mae would have to learn he was not to be toyed with. "Do you understand me Mae?"

Still not looking at him, Mae jerked from his grasp and wrapped her arms around her midsection and began to shake harder. "So we are back to calling me Mae now?" Her words were harsh. "Of course I understand. *It* will not happen again. Ever." She went to walk away without picking up her skirts. As a result, the clothing caught on a low branch, and she yanked at them with force. The clothing released, and she lost her balance. Before she could tumble to the ground, John caught her against him and almost cursed out loud at the awakening in his body from the feel of the soft plush curves.

"I'm fine. I'll go now," Mae pushed away, but he held her in place.

"Mae look…"

"Don't say another word. There is nothing else I want to hear on the subject. Not now."

"Fine, then go, but be warned next time, I'm leaving you, even if it's out in the middle of nowhere. I'll break my word to Miss Lady." Rounded eyes swung to him, and she bowed her head so her hair would conceal her face. "John, stop." She made her way back toward the wagon.

He'd caught a glimpse of her bruised jawline and a split on her bottom lip. He caught up to her and blocked her path, his hands on her forearms "My God, what happened to you? You're hurt."

Her hands flat on his chest and twisting her face away, she pushed against him. "Let me go."

"Not until you let me see your face." He glanced over toward the wagon to see that Jefferson had his back to them, carrying the bedrolls to the wagon. "Mae please, let me see." He loosened his hold on her, keeping his fingers curled around her biceps. Until he saw it all, he would not release her arms.

Head held high, she finally turned and met his gaze. In addition to the bruising and the lip injury, there were scratches on her neck.

Her lips twisted into a sneer, and she spoke slowly past clenched teeth. "Let me go John."

"Why didn't you call for help?" He refused to release her until she would answer.

Finally she relented, her shoulder's slumping in surrender. "I did call for you. You didn't come." Seeming to be startled by her words, she gasped and closed her eyes.

"Did he…"

"No I fought him off," she interrupted her eyes focused past his shoulders. "Now let me go." The whispered words were barely audible.

John finally released her, and with a quick jerk, she picked up her skirts to avoid the low branches and made her way back toward the wagon.

She'd needed his help. Had called for him the night before. The thought sickened John. One thing he could never stand was for a man to hurt a woman. How had she managed to fight him off? His gut clenched, thinking how terrified she must have been to call for his help. He understood her anger at him for not coming to her aid.

Heat infused his body at the thought of Jefferson accosting Mae right under his nose, while he lay there close enough to help her. Instead, he'd supposed the worst and ignored the sounds. A red fog colored his vision until it became like a long tunnel, everything dark except for the lighted center. The only thing he saw clearly was Jefferson, who now stood next to the wagon glaring at Mae as she stopped walking and stood next to the horses.

With long strides, he went straight to where Jefferson stood and before he knew it, John had two fistfuls of the man's shirt and was dragging Jefferson away from the wagon.

With a loud growl, John drew back his fist. The solid hit took Jefferson by surprise, and the younger man landed flat on his back with his legs and arms outstretched. Without giving the coward the opportunity to get his wits, John lifted him by the collar and punched him again and again. Jefferson growled and bucked him off.

"What you hittin' me for Captain McClain?" The younger man attempted to scramble away. "She asked for it. She ain't nothing but a whore. We both know it."

John tackled him, and once again they began to hit at each other. The pair tumbled one over the other throwing punches until Mae screamed, startling them to a stop.

"Enough! Stop at once before you kill him." Her face impassive in spite of her high-pitched statement, she stood a short distance away with one hand flat on her chest, her face flushed.

"Let's go, we need to keep moving."

John held Jefferson down on the ground. "You will remain here. I don't give a damn how you get where you're going," He got up leaving the young man on his side panting. "Get your belongings off my wagon now."

Jefferson scrambled to his feet and attempted to move toward the wagon, only to bend over and throw up.

Mae watched him with a dispassionate expression, her eyebrows lifted. Then she gave John a once over as he approached. "You need to go to the stream and wash up. Then we'll go to the nearest town and drop him off." She motioned with her head toward Jefferson, who was now an unseemly shade of green and sat on the ground leaning against the wagon wheel. "He's in no shape to be left here alone."

John approached her. "Mae I'm sorry. You called me, and I didn't come to help you. I should have been there for you instead…"

"Instead you thought the worst of me. Go wash up so we can leave please." She went toward the front of the wagon giving him her back.

Guilt crushed down on his shoulders as John walked away to do as she bid. With his energy depleted and his leg throbbing, he collapsed at the water's edge when reaching it and splashed cold stream water onto his face. The burning cuts on his hands and face numbed at the coolness of the water, relieving some of the ache. He pulled off his shirt, boots and pants, not caring at this point if Mae watched and waded further into the water. With eyes closed, he dove in and then surfaced to float on his back.

Anger clung to his gut, and his stomach clenched with a sickness from letting Mae down. Not protecting her like he'd promised Miss Lady. So soon into the trip, he'd already failed. He'd also thought the worst of her while Mae off an assault.

John dove underwater once again then surfaced and swam to the shore. When he reached his clothes, he began to dress while praying Jefferson was in the back of the wagon when he returned to it hidden from his sight. He was not sure how long it would be before he could keep from reacting. Yes it was best if he didn't see the bastard right now.

It was going to be another long day.

Chapter Six

"*LISTEN HERE LITTLE Maebelle and you remember what I tell you. Words are men's greatest weapon. If you let what somebody says cut into you, it can tear you wide open. You gonna have to be strong and always hold your head high.*" *Miss Lady held out her hand, palm up. It was empty. "Take this from my hand."* *Mae's small fingers curled over it, picking up the imaginary item. "Now push it into your chest." Mae pretended to push it into her body and giggled at Miss Lady's pleased expression. "That's a good girl, now you got strength inside you. As long as you do, cain't nobody hurt you." Miss Lady pressed her hand over Mae's on her small chest. "Do you understand?" Mae nodded not quite understanding. "Now repeat after me. I am a strong, valuable lady. Repeat it." Mae began repeating the words. "I am a strong, valuable lady. I am a strong, valuable lady."*

Mae clung to the words Miss Lady ensured she repeated many times over the years. Then John rounded the wagon and forced Jefferson from the back.

"I can't believe you're leaving me here and taking a two-bit whore's side." Jefferson's arms waved wildly and his eyes bulged in his mottled swollen face.

They'd made it to the outskirts of a particularly small town, and John stopped the wagon. It was close enough that Jefferson could walk, yet far enough it would take him some time to arrive.

The men stood a few feet away from the wagon facing off. John towered over the shorter male. He stood taut, his features tight with anger.

Although the younger male's words were nothing new, Mae forced her attention away from the duo to the tiny town. In the distance, Mae made out only a couple of people exiting what looked to be a small general store. Other than another man walking into what looked to be a shop of some sort, no other people were present.

With a hand over her brow to shade her eyes, she turned to see Jefferson direct an angry glare at her. "She ain't worth it Captain McClain. You'll find out soon enough. I 'spose you already got plans, as it's a long lonely road to Texas…" The young man's words stopped when John grabbed him up by his collar and pulled him face-to-face with him.

Mae strained to hear John's reply to Jefferson's exclamation. Whatever John replied in a low growl to the now struggling man was too soft for Mae to make out the words. Not that it mattered. The only reason she remained on the wagon rather than Jefferson was because John gave his word to Miss Lady, and if nothing else, he was a man of his word, otherwise she'd bet a large amount it would be her standing on the side of the road. She doubted he felt badly for what happened to her. He'd actually thought she'd willingly lay with Jefferson.

When Mae looked over her shoulder one last time, she saw

John push a sputtering Jefferson away and walk toward the wagon. A passive expression did not hide the clench of his jaw and brightness of his eyes. When he climbed up to sit beside her, she kept her back straight and eyes ahead as the seat shifted under John's weight.

From under her lashes, she spied John's grim expression, his face sharp angles from the tight lips and drawn brow. He snapped the reins, and the horses moved the wagon forward at quickened pace into the town. Just a few minutes later, he pulled to a stop in front of the general store. Without looking at her, he jumped down and tethered the horses. "Would you like to come inside with me?"

Mae shook her head. She preferred not to face people with her bruised face and cut lip. Once left alone, she leaned out to look back, nervous that Jefferson would come up from behind her. It was obvious the man had a mean streak, probably kept a grudge too. With his pack over one shoulder, the young male headed toward town. Fortunately he was still far enough she couldn't make out his features. Relieved he seemed to be taking his time, she peered through one of the shop's windows. John stood at the counter, hat in one hand and a parcel in the other. When he turned to head out, Mae resumed her perusal of the road ahead.

The wagon shifted when John climbed into the wagon just a few moments later. He replaced his hat on his head and held out the small parcel to her. "It's some hard candy. For you." Mae's mouth watered, yet she took her time opening the parcel, careful not to tear the paper too much and then offered it to him. Once he popped the candy into his mouth, John grabbed the reins. "The shopkeeper told me there's a boarding house a few hours ride from here. We should reach it by nightfall. I know you'd appreciate spending the night on a real bed for a change. Is it to your liking?"

"Yes, it would be wonderful." Mae almost cried at the combination of the sweet candy in her mouth and the thought of a warm bath followed by a soft bed.

The reins tight, he snapped the horses to get moving. "Well, seems we got us a place to head to then." The crinkle of her closing the paper over the candy caught his eye. "May I have another one please?" She shared his peace offering, and he took one more. "Thank you."

They rode in silence for a several hours before John brought the wagon to a stop. He climbed down and checked her horse's hooves. "This one seems to be limping." He patted Mae's horse on the rump. "I don't notice anything amiss, although it's better to be safe. I'm going to unhitch them and take a better look. You may want to take advantage, we won't stop again."

Mae scrambled down and made her way to some trees for privacy. Once in the shade of the trees, she leaned against a tree and closed her eyes. Who was John McClain? Why did he treat her with disdain one moment and buy her candy the next? Guilt. He felt guilty for what Jefferson had done. It was the only answer she could think of.

After relieving herself, Mae made her way back toward the wagon. The horses were once again ready to go, and John stood at her side waiting to assist her. Their eyes met. His dark gray eyes seemed to bore into hers, and for a brief moment everything stood still. Mae took a shaky breath at the warm sensation when his hand touched her elbow to push her up into her seat. Road weariness was the only explanation she could find for her reaction. John McClain would never consider her more than a burden.

To him, she was nothing more than a common whore.

Soon they were on the road again, the horses trotting along perfectly. Her back stiff, Mae stretched and moaned. It was too soon into the journey to be so sore. They were not even half way. How would she survive until Texas?

Twilight's long shadows began to fall over the wagon, Mae shivered in the cool evening air. "How long before we arrive?" Hours earlier, she'd given up pretending to be strong, too exhausted to care and had slumped over, her head on John's shoulder. "Maybe we should just stop and make camp. I am so tired."

John's shoulder moved up and down when he shrugged. "I promised you a bed Mae, and you should have one tonight. We've got another hour or so before night falls. Let's give it a bit."

How could he remain so strong? Probably due to his years in the Calvary, riding for days on end, with little in the way of accommodations or regular meals even. Truth be told, she'd not slept a wink after Jefferson's attack. Afraid he'd return, she'd kept an eye on the back of the wagon. If only she could relax more, understand John.

Seeming to read her mind, he began to talk. "On one of my assignments, two men and I spent so many days out in the wilderness chasing after a deserter we became delusional. We were so hungry. The sounds of our stomachs growling became so loud, I was sure if we neared the man he'd hear us coming." He chuckled and Mae got the feeling he could see the scene he spoke of. "We spotted some wild fowl and had a feast that night. For some reason, the next day Corporal Harrison began to cluck like a chicken in the direction of another soldier. The man, a sergeant, lost his temper and dove from his horse to grab at him. Well, I don't know how they managed it, but both got all tangled up and ended up hanging upside down from Harrison's horse."

Mae giggled in spite of the tiredness, thinking of the poor men hanging upside down on a horse. "What happened to them? Did they get hurt?"

"Not really, except Harrison did get a black eye. I guess his face rammed into the horse's leg. I suppose the horse was too startled to move, and it gave several of us time to help them get off the horse." He shook his head at the memory. "When I asked Harrison why he was clucking, he said it was a joke. He'd overheard the sergeant tell another soldier he had a hard time plucking fowls' feathers and then eating them."

It was the most he'd spoken to her, the deep timber of his voice soothing her. She opened her mouth to ask him another question in an effort to keep the conversation going, but he spoke again.

"There it is," John told her pointing. "Looks like the place the shopkeeper told me about."

Suddenly aware that she still laid her head on his shoulder, she straightened and her gaze scanned the building. It was a modest two-story house, a bit smaller than hers. Smoke from the chimney promised a warm interior. Light streamed from the windows. When they neared, the front door opened, and a large barrel-chested man came out to greet them. His eyes lit on Mae's bruised face for only a beat before he rounded to John's side of the wagon. An easy smile curved his lips. "The wife saw y'all comin' and sent me out to greet ya." With a hearty laugh, he shook his head. "Mighty bossy for a such a tiny woman. I'm Clark Clearwater. The wife's name is Beth Ann." The men shook hands, and John looked to her and her eyes widened.

Without speaking, both realized they would not be able to stay the night. An unmarried couple would not be welcomed into this or any respectable home. It took several gulps for the lump of sadness to finally get past her throat.

John turned back to the man. "John and Maebelle McClain. The missus and I are hopeful you have a spare room for us. She's had a hard time of it. We were accosted a ways back."

The man's scrutiny made Mae shift. "Well goodness sakes, I'm glad you weren't hurt too bad."

"I ran him off," John told the man, and Mr. Clearwater's eyes lit on the bruising on John's jaw and then the cuts on his knuckles. "It would be nice to get some safe shelter for a night."

"Of course, of course," Mr. Clearwater helped John with the bags while Mae made her way to the front door. A short woman greeted her at the front door. Her graying hair pulled back into a tight bun brought attention to her round face softened by a spray of freckles across her nose. "Well come on in. I know you must be exhausted."

"Dead on my feet," Mae admitted. "Although I could collapse easily, I desperately need a bath before I could lay in a clean bed."

THE BED LOOMED larger than life, and the more time passed the more it took her attention. Mae sat in the steamy tub and stared at the sizeable four-poster bed. Earlier, she and John stood next to each other awkwardly while Mrs. Clearwater showed them the room. The woman did not seem to notice anything amiss and had briskly called for the bath water to be brought by a young man who looked to be their teenage son. After the lad finally left, John excused himself to give her privacy. So intent on getting into the warm water she didn't even consider the ramifications of their lie. Not until now.

Well there was nothing to be done about it now. Surely the man didn't mean to sleep in the bed with her. She'd offer him the bed, especially after noticing his limp after the brawl with Jefferson. He needed to rest, ensure his leg did not get infected or cause him to fall ill again. She'd sleep on the floor. A couple of blankets and one of the pillows on the rug would still be more comfortable than the back of the wagon. She rose from the bath to change and descend to join John for dinner. Before leaving the room, she pulled her hair down along the sides of her face before pulling it back. The style hid the bruising on her jawline. Not much could be done about the other wounds, although her lip was barely swollen now, and beneath her eye, the slash of purple had decreased.

When Mae descended the stairs, there were several other guests along with John already gathered around a square wooden table. Conversation stopped, and everyone turned to look at her. With a forced smile, she moved forward, keeping her eyes on John. With a grim expression in place, he stood and pulled a chair for her. Once she sat, he lowered into the chair next to hers and introduced her once again as his wife.

AFTER DINNER, JOHN paced outside the house, ignoring the pulses of protest from his leg. Did the woman even understand what she did to him? To other men in any room she entered? Dinner had been the longest of his life, the unfortunate closeness of their bodies made it hard for their legs not to occasionally touch. And the way she looked. John almost grabbed her to drag her back upstairs. She was not dressed immodest, but even if clad in a flour sack, the woman commanded the attention of every male in a room.

The other four guests were men, and it became very hard to keep from demanding they stop staring at her. Mae, either used to it or oblivious, had been the picture of grace, taking time to speak to each of them until they were practically eating out of her hand. John clenched his jaw. Of course she did. It was what she did for a living.

Currently she was preparing for bed while he gave her a few minutes of solitude. Too tired to remain upright, she'd surprised him when her head leaned onto his shoulder. He hated to admit how good the closeness felt, how strong it made him feel. Without realizing it, he'd slowed the horses, stretching the time until they arrived. He had to get all the confusing emotions under control before they got on the road again and spending unending hours alone. One of the guests stepped outside and nodded at him before moving away to light a cigarette. John wasn't in the mood to start a conversation so he went back inside.

John made his way up the stairs, each step matching the deep breaths he took. What now? He was overthinking things as usual. Surely they could maintain their distance in the large bedroom. They were adults, and he was responsible for keeping her safe.

A charge.

No, it was his duty.

The intimacy of the interior did little to settle his mind. A lamp cast a soft light in the room. Mae was bent at the waist placing a blanket on the rug. Dressed in a floor length, long sleeved nightgown, she swung to face him, her eyes wide. "Oh goodness, you startled me John. I didn't hear footsteps."

He eyed the blankets she was arranging on the floor. "What are you doing? I will take care of it. Lie down and get some rest."

She straightened. "John, I think it's best if I sleep on the floor." He started to argue, but she moved closer and he could only swallow. The light from the lamp caused for her entire body to be silhouetted. Long legs and the soft curves of her outlined for him to see. "…you've been limping. It's more pronounced today, and after sleeping on the hard ground for days, it makes more sense." He finally listened to her words and realized Mae was unaware of how sheer her gown was. Or was she?

Forcing his eyes away from her, he grunted and went to pour a glass of water. "Damn woman do you have to make every thing so difficult?" Her irritated sniff brought his gaze back to her.

With her nose in the air, she threw the blanket at him and moved to the bed. "You know what John. Sleep in the barn for all I care. I'm trying to be nice, making sure you're leg…is…oh never mind." The last word came out more of a growl.

"Mae? I, er…you were…are nice."

"Forget it John. Do what you want, I'm going to sleep. I'm too tired to deal with you right now." When she noticed he'd neared, she dropped her arms to her sides and didn't move away. Her bright emerald eyes met his. "Let's just admit how bad of an idea this entire trip is. We can inquire at the next town about a stagecoach…I can…"

His mouth crushed hers, surprising him far more than her. She didn't move away when he placed his hands on both side of her face holding her in place, not wanting her to. She tasted like everything he ever imagined since meeting her, sweet and fiery. Her hands covered his, and Mae returned his kiss. It took all he had within him to keep from moaning.

Past the point of rational thought, he pressed his tongue to her lips and her mouth opened, inviting him in. Minutes passed, lacing one to another with only the sound of their breathing and suckling. The silken tresses fell down her back, and John smoothed them back from her face. When his hand slid to the small of her back, she pulled away and stepped back. Her wide eyes locked to his face, she moved further away and rounded the bed. Without a word, she pulled the remaining blanket away and lay down with her back to him and pulled the blankets up over her shoulders.

"I'm sorry Mae, I didn't mean to…"

"No explanation necessary. Of course you didn't John. Why in the world would you?"

Not sure what could be said to make things better, he began to arrange the blankets on the floor. He removed his clothes and lay down.

In the darkness, John listened to Mae's breathing until he was sure she slept, then got up and went to blow out the lamp. He glanced at her and couldn't help but wonder what would happen to her. In sleep, her beauty could only be described as pure. Innocent, the furthest word one would normally use when referring to Mae. Desirable, intriguing and ultimately dangerous, those were a much better fit.

He focused on her pursed lips and without thought touched his own. The light reflected a shiny tear sliding down from the corner of her eye. She cried in her sleep. Had he caused it?

Once again the heaviness fell upon him at wondering if he was indeed the cause of her sorrow. The first reaction was to reach out and wipe the errant tear. Instead John blew out the lamp instead. On the bedroll, he stared up at the ceiling. From now on, he'd make more of an effort to keep a distance from her. The kiss was a mistake. Now he'd gotten the curiosity out of his system, it would be easier to control any impulses in the future. Yet down deep he knew it was a lie; he'd never forget the taste of Mae's kiss.

THE NEXT MORNING, Mae ate breakfast downstairs while John bathed. Mrs. Clearwater poured coffee into a large sturdy mug for her. She'd lingered in bed as long as possible enjoying the comfort of the soft mattress. When she'd first awakened, the sight of a sleeping John kept her attention. On his back, he was sprawled on the blankets, his breathing even, on hand curled under his jaw. Thankfully, guilt didn't assail, as he seemed as comfortable as she on the downy bed coverings she'd shed from the bed.

Mrs. Clearwater placed a plate replete with eggs and potatoes before the woman smiled brightly at Mae's enthusiastic eating.

"Is there a stagecoach stop in the next town?" Mae blurted between bites, realizing her mistake when the woman's concerned gaze focused on her bruised lip.

"No dear there isn't, not a regular stop anyway. The route runs south of here, so you'd have to double back a ways." She looked over her shoulder toward the staircase. "Does he beat you often?"

Mae met the woman's eyes evenly. "No John does not hit me. He'd never lay a hand on me. Thank you for your concern, but we really were accosted." She waved away the woman's apology. "I asked because I planned to recommend your home to my—my mother when she travels to visit me."

"Oh dear, that would be lovely. If she comes through here, I'd love to meet her."

John descended the stairs, his eyes immediately seeking her. "Good morning." With wet hair brushed away from his face and a clean shirt, he looked refreshed and unfortunately as handsome as ever.

Both women responded and Mrs. Clearwater hustled to the stove to fetch his breakfast.

"There isn't a stagecoach stop along this road," Mae told him keeping her eyes on her coffee cup and her voice to a whisper.

"I will get you to Texas Mae," he replied in a low tone. "It's going to be fine, I will ensure nothing else will happen between us to make this trip harder than it needs to be."

She hoped so. Because it was already proving to be an ordeal.

Chapter Seven

WITH A DEEP sigh, Mae watched as John returned from behind some trees. It had been two days since they'd left the Clearwater's house, and she had to acknowledge the overnight stay there helped her rest up considerably. They'd maintained a cordial existence between them with no talk of the kiss. A sort of interesting mutual understanding kept the hours together from turning awkward. Yes, as long as they stayed a safe distance away, they could co-exist without incident. Admittedly her mind revisited the kiss on occasion. However, she was able to rein her thoughts under control while in John's presence.

Mae shifted closer to the campfire and poked at a piece of wood pushing it toward the flames. Without looking, she sensed John settling onto the log next to her. They'd avoided any conversation about anything personal. Actually, they'd barely spoken more than necessary, so his question startled her.

"Why are you really going to see your father?"

Because Miss Lady insisted, would have kept at her until she'd run out of excuses for not going. "I suppose it's more curiosity than anything else. Miss Lady seems to think he owes me an explanation for never having anything to do with me.

Plus he's very ill. It may be my last opportunity to speak with him." She also wanted to hear his reasons for not seeking her out.

"But you don't agree he owes you?" he urged her to continue.

"No." She shrugged keeping her eyes on the rising flares. "I can understand his decision to not marry my mother and stay in Virginia."

"Because she was a prostitute?"

"No, it was not the reason. My mother was not a prostitute when she became pregnant with me. It was out of necessity to raise me and support us that she turned our home into what it is today. She not only had to find a way to provide for me after her father died, but also for Miss Lady and Lucinda, who was also just a babe." Not wanting him to know how much his assumptions affected her, she kept her voice even. "My father had his reasons nonetheless, and I'm not sure I care to know what they are."

"I understand," John replied, his gray eyes searching her face. "Do you remember him?"

Why did he want to continue this conversation? "Barely. He came to see me when I was between three and four. He brought me a doll and gave mother some money for me. I suppose he came to see if I resembled him, to ensure I was truly his daughter." She decided to trudge on so his questions would hopefully end. "Mother said he was shocked at how much I favored him. Yet when she begged him to take me and raise me away from the life she'd carved out, once again he refused her. Said he had a wife and was starting a new life, had no room for a child born out of wedlock. So he left and never contacted me again. Until now."

Emotions she could not discern flickered in his eyes, his brow knit he studied the flames for a few minutes. "So then it was just your mother and you? What happened to her? Where is she now?"

More questions and this time she pondered whether to reply or not. Her mother, she rarely allowed herself to think about the woman and her tragic life. "My mother grew more sad, melancholy after my father's last visit. I believe he was the love of her life, as she never allowed another person to get close to her."

"Not even you." John stated, his eyes never leaving her face. "She left you?"

With a bitter chuckle, she replied. "No, not even me, kept me at an arms distance. And no she did not leave, not physically anyway. She became addicted to opium, a way to escape I suppose. She threw herself into making money, working and hiring more girls. Although she had lovers, she never permitted a man to lay with her for more than one night. She had no repeat customers. Soon her addiction to the drug took its toll, and she rarely left her bedroom. She died when I was thirteen, in her room. Miss Lady raised me after."

John reached for her, and she braced for it. Since the night at the Clearwater's, how she'd ached for his arms to surround her and the warmth of his body to sooth her. As if shocked by what he was about to do, he pulled back and stood instead. He looked away toward the horizon away from her. "Why did you choose to continue in the business?"

Ah, the reason for his withdrawal. This time the familiar pang of being judged stung. She'd be damned before he'd know it. She forced her words to come out matter-of-factly and shrugged once again. "I didn't know anything else. As my relatives in Northern Virginia disowned my mother, I had no family, other than a colored woman, her daughter. My life was the thriving brothel. Perhaps I could have taken the money we'd saved and moved away. Nonetheless, I figured sooner or later, unless I moved across the country, someone would recognize or remember me. The inevitable will happen. I made my choice and continued the life my mother carved out for me. I've come to the conclusion and accepted not to aspire to a normal life."

"I suppose not."

His simple statement pierced deeper than she expected and Mae stood. "I'm going to clean up. It's getting near sundown." She stumbled toward the tree line, tears stinging her eyes. The truth always hurt, its bite relentless and searing. John would never see her as anything other than a prostitute. It was not just his judgment, but his reaction, which made her clench her jaw in frustration. What the heck was the matter with her? It wasn't like her to be so sensitive. The sooner this damn trip was over, the better off she'd be.

The coolness of the water was refreshing, and Mae lingered, walking along the shoreline. Why did she sometimes dream of a different life? It made no sense to allow herself the illusion of an impossible outcome. This time away from her home and the familiar was beginning to affect her in a way, which was not good. Vulnerability was a dangerous thing for her.

Returning toward the campsite, the sound of horses brought her out of her musings, and she peered around a tree to see John walking toward a newly arrived couple perched high on a wagon. A man and woman who looked to be in their thirties. The man climbed down and extended his hand, and the men shook. The woman, a brunette wearing a bonnet that obstructed her face, looked on as the man motioned to her with his hand.

Mae remained at a distance, not sure she was in the mood to deal with strangers. The men talked for a few minutes, seeming to come to some sort of agreement when they shook hands again.

Her back straight, Mae forced a neutral look when John turned toward where she stood and waved her over. Her stomach pitched at the matching expectant expressions on the couple's face. What agreement had John just made? Would she travel with them to Texas so he could leave her?

When she finally approached, the woman now stood next to the man, his arm protectively around her shoulders. When Mae neared them, the man's eyes widened just a bit, enough Mae noticed. How she hated the reaction she brought out in men. It was always the same, quickly masked interest like now or a leering expectation. She plastered a fake smile on her face and closed the distance until she stood next to John.

"Mae, this is Mister and Misses Jacobs." John motioned to the couple smiling at her.

The man spoke first. "I'm Ryan, and this is my wife Patricia." He held out his hand, and she noted his eyes were now gentle when meeting hers. When she held her hand out, his fingers wrapped around it. "It's a pleasure to make your acquaintance Missus McClain."

Her back stiffened, and she refused to look at John. The woman's smile became brighter when Mae turned to her. Instead of shaking her hand, the tiny brunette threw her arms around Mae and embraced her. "I am so happy your husband has agreed to allow us to ride with you the rest of the way to Texas. I've been so lonely for female companionship." The woman gushed. Mae noted upon closer inspection Patricia Jacobs was a pretty woman, her dark brown eyes seeming to fill her face, a sprinkle of freckles across her nose making her seem young.

"Oh," Mae replied finally meeting John's steady gaze. "Well welcome. Please, come sit by the fire. Are you hungry? There is some stew left."

"No thank you and please call me Patty." The women stayed close to Mae's side as they walked away from the men. "We ate not so long ago and were looking for a place to make camp and spend the night away near water when we happened upon your husband and the wagon."

While the men unhitched the horses and led them to the nearby creek, Mae sat back down in the same place where she'd just gotten up from minutes earlier. Patty Jacobs eyed her with curiosity. "Your husband told us you are newlyweds. It must be hard for you to be on such a hard trip so soon after being wed."

"Yes, well it wasn't exactly planned," Mae started and then wondered how much John had said. "Nonetheless, it has not been too dreadful."

The men returned and the four of them drank coffee, discussing the travel ahead. Finally Ryan stood and stretched. "Well folks, we appreciate it plenty you're allowing us to ride together. For safety reasons, I feel better knowing there are two men to keep these beautiful ladies protected." His eyes lingered on his wife, and Mae had to look away at the affection glances crossed between them.

"You told them we were married?" Mae asked, as the couple disappeared into the back of their wagon. "How are we going to pull this off for the rest of the journey?"

"I had to. I agree with Ryan. The deeper we get to untamed territory, the safer it will be with two men. Besides, he is a clergyman," John replied as if it explained everything. He stood dusting his pants. "I'll get my bedroll."

"Don't you think they will suspect you lied when you sleep out here, and I sleep in the back of the wagon?"

He hadn't thought. She could tell by the way his eyes flew to their wagon and back to her. "I...er...damn." John slumped back down. "I don't know what I was thinking. I should have told them we were brother and sister."

"Right." Mae stood and looked down at him. "Come John, it's getting late. Let's go to sleep. I promise not to touch you." She smirked at his shocked expression and walked away.

John was smart enough to stay outside the wagon until she settled onto the makeshift bed in the back of the wagon. She'd pushed as many goods as she could to the front to allow more space sideways. Her stomach flipped when he climbed in and sat next to her. Without preamble, he removed his shirt and lay with his back to her while leaving plenty of space between them. "Good night Mae."

"Good night John," She replied and lay on her back as well, listening to his breathing until a soft snore sounded. Then she finally was able to relax. Through the darkness, she couldn't make out much, but she noted how, up close, his back was quite wide, tapering to a slender waist. Heat emanated from his large body, and she wanted nothing more than to snuggle against it for warmth. Instead she pulled a blanket over him and a separate one over herself.

What would the morning bring? They still had another two weeks of travel, and somehow they would have to keep up the pretense of being married. Of all the things she'd endured so far, this would be the hardest. The stagecoach would have been a lot less trouble.

She'd been smitten with him upon meeting him five years ago when he arrived to Widow's Peak, and it lasted through the years and his long absences when the regiment was sent away. Each time he returned to town, she'd found a way to catch glimpses of him in town or when he'd ridden by to corral up his men. Rarely when he did enter her house to see about his men, she'd memorized each word he spoke and each expression.

Her feelings had changed over the years. No longer a young impressionable girl, she now knew without a doubt and no matter how much she tried to tell herself otherwise, she loved John McClain. He was her impossible. She'd accepted it long ago and kept the feelings locked inside. If only she keep it from affecting her in any manner when near him. Her brain understood the danger of it, the hurt would come from the feeling, of course her foolish heart didn't know any better. It didn't understand the sentiment would never be returned. If anything the next few days would give her some memories to keep for the rest of her life. She relaxed and closed her eyes to await slumber.

A SUNRAY BROKE through the cover on the back of the wagon crossing over her face and Mae's eyes flickered open. John was now sprawled on his back; one arm over his eyes the other across his chest. Mae studied the tendrils of hair splayed on the blanket next to her. His hair was too long; maybe she'd ask if he would like her to cut it. She reached over to touch it when he spoke and she drew her hand back.

"Good morning." The grogginess of his voice told her he's just woken.

"How did you know I was awake?"

He huffed with impatience. "Your breathing pattern changed." John's sat up and reached for his shirt. "Best get on with it. We need to be on the road." He grumbled and climbed out of the wagon putting distance between them.

"Well now I know you're not in the best mood in the mornings." She called after him. "God, I'm so tired of traveling," Mae mumbled and rolled onto his empty spot wrapping the discarded blanket over her head. She inhaled his scent, and closed her eyes.

Chapter Eight

J OHN PRACTICALLY SPRINTED to the creek. It was torture for him to lie next to Mae and not make her his. His entire body demanded it. When he reached the water and splashed the cold liquid onto his face, his breathing hitched from the shock. How would he survive another night, much less several next to her and not touch her? She'd made it easy for him the night before by bantering and then ensuring there was more space. It wasn't enough, as he'd woken several times during the night when they'd touched, either her leg moving against him or his hand against her back.

He groaned and ran his hand down his front rubbing away the throbbing between his legs. When it didn't help at all, he yanked his clothes off and sank into the creek. The frigid water took his breath away, but the result was exactly what he needed. It would only be a few minutes before he had to surface, but he hoped it would serve to keep him from embarrassing himself in front of the Jacobs'.

Shivering, he dressed and went to see about breakfast. Nearing the camp, he saw the Jacobs were already up and getting the fire started. Ryan placed the coffee pot onto the flames while his wife went past John toward the creek. "Good morning John," She murmured looking up at him. "Is Mae up yet?"

"Yes," John replied looking to his wagon, the curtain remained closed. "I will check on her."

"Ryan said you planned to leave at sunrise, so we're ready when you are." She smiled and continued on her way.

He neared his wagon and looked over his shoulder to note Ryan watched him. Without preamble he pulled the curtain aside. "Mae, are you up? We are leaving in a few minutes."

Mae sat up, blonde curls tumbled down past her shoulders, her lips pursed and brows drawn in a frown. "Oh John, I am so tired," she rubbed her eyes, and her blanket fell down past her breasts, the thin material of her nightgown doing little to conceal what lay beneath. She didn't seem to notice and made her way to the back of the wagon toward him.

"Where are you going?" John held his hands up to stop her.

She gave him a wide-eyed look. "To the creek. I have to wash up, get ready to go. Remember what you said? 'Get on with it'," Mae replied in a slow deliberate tone. She tried to push his hands aside. "John, I'm in no mood for whatever you are doing, let me by."

"The Jacobs are here. And well your nightgown…it's a bit sheer."

"Oh dear!" A bright red flush covered her face, and she fell back onto her bottom crossing her arms over her chest to conceal the most beautiful sight he'd seen in a long time, which unfortunately made him wonder if another dip in the creek was required.

"Once you are dressed, come have coffee," he muttered and

went to find some for himself.

"I'm not ready to get up," Mae grumbled and kicked with her heel at the flooring for emphasis. "This has to be Miss Lady's worse idea ever."

"WHY ARE YOU going to Texas, John?" Mae asked the following night as they lay in the wagon, in the darkness, trying their best not to touch. "Is that where you are from?"

Her warm breath tickled his shoulder and he fought not to turn to her. He supposed it was only fair she asked questions; after all he'd asked a lot of her. "No, I am from Northern Virginia. I am looking for someone in Texas."

"Do you plan to return to Virginia after?" She adjusted the blanket around herself, ensuring it covered up to her neck. He found her attempt at modesty endearing. "I don't know. I may stay in Texas for a bit. Although my parents are getting older and may need help with the press."

"Press?"

"Yes my father owns a printing press. It's what I did before joining the cavalry." He waited until she replied.

"Interesting." She let out a soft breath. "Who are you looking for?"

He was not quite sure how to answer her question. Who indeed? "A man, a woman and a child."

Mae turned to him and in the dimness he could make out her wide stare. "Are they outlaws? Running from the law with a child? How sad."

"No, I am no longer in the cavalry and not seeking to bring outlaws into custody. I am seeking the woman and child…my child."

"What?" Mae screeched and sat up with a jolt. "Oh God. Your wife? Did the man kidnap them?"

"No she went with him voluntarily."

"Is she your wife?"

John didn't want to delve into the subject. He wasn't even sure the child was his and if the information he had would even result in finding them. He should have kept it all to himself. "Good night Mae." He attempted to roll to his side, but her hand grabbed his arm. His lack of reply seemed to have answered the question in Mae's mind.

"Oh my God," she hissed. "You are married, and you didn't see fit to tell me."

It didn't register to him until the second hit, she attempted to slap him and missed.

"Stop it now Mae." John grabbed for her hands and held her against him until she stopped struggling. "Be quiet now or the Jacobs will hear."

"I don't care," Mae told him not bothering to keep her voice down. "How could you keep this secret?" She began to struggle again, this time he released her and she scrambled out of the wagon.

"Damn it." John got up and climbed down. He made out her white nightgown as she ran toward the creek and started to call after her. Then Ryan stuck his head out of the back of his wagon.

"Is everything all right?"

John shook his head. "She's…very angry with me right now." He looked to see Mae had disappeared from sight.

"Well go after her, and apologize John, you can't let her go around stumbling in the dark. She may get hurt," John stated matter-of-factly. "See you in the morning."

"Yeah," John replied and went to find Mae.

It didn't take long to find her. She sat on the ground next to a small tree. With her arms around her knees her cheek against the top of her knees. Although she didn't seem to be crying, John approached her slowly and crouched down. "Mae you cannot stay out here. Come back to the wagon. It's cold out here."

"No. Just go John. I need to think." She sniffed, and he realized he was wrong and she was crying.

He sat next to her and placed his arm around her, surprised when she didn't push away. Not sure what to say, he did what Ryan suggested. "I'm sorry."

"What will your wife think when she finds out we traveled together? You with a prostitute, a woman of no morals."

"Don't call yourself that."

"Why not? It's what you consider me. You don't think of me as otherwise do you?"

John took her face with both hands and turned her to face him. "I think of you as a beautiful strong woman."

"I can't with a clear conscience pretend to be married to you to the Jacobs. I wish you'd not told them we are married." She sniffed and wiped angrily at her face.

"I would be forced to do it regardless, because we are on this journey together without a chaperone. I would do it to protect people from judging you."

Noting she shivered, he sat placed his other arm around her pulling her close.

She sniffed again and laid her head on his shoulder. "Who is she? Why is your wife in Texas?"

Not ready to divulge more than necessary until he found out the reason for the woman being in Texas, his reply was short. "Carla is not my wife Mae. She's someone I knew. A woman who is going to explain many things to me when I get there."

He pulled Mae up with him. "Come on Mae, let's get some rest."

"I can't." She pulled out of his reach. "I'm simpering like a fool, over what I'm not sure. This trip, this constant tiredness is affecting me in ways I'm not comfortable with. I will remain out here."

Why would she feel this way, after all? Why would his being married cause her any duress? Surely she'd lain with married men or men in relationships before? John tried to come up with a way to reason with her, but was at a loss. He failed at controlling his temper. "Damn it Mae you are being unreasonable, now come on. I won't allow you to remain out here alone."

She stood her ground, arms crossed, her bottom lip out and her brows knit. "No."

The urge to grab her and throw her over his shoulder became strong, however he held a reign on his anger. "Fine you know what, I won't force you to do anything you don't want to." The cold air made him angrier. "Ryan knows were are fighting, so I'll sleep on the bedroll by the campfire tonight. Go on to the wagon and sleep, I won't go near it. Not tonight. But tomorrow I will."

She eyed him for a few moments; her gaze filled with mistrust, then Mae got to her feet rounded him and headed back towards the wagon.

John remained rooted to the spot. Now what? Why didn't he keep Carla's existence to himself?

His leg throbbed and he bent to rub the wound on his calf. Another thing to thank Carla for. The woman was proving to be a colossal mistake.

Tomorrow he'd see about setting things straight with Mae. That her anger bothered him so much made him ponder his feelings for her. She'd become important to him. It was certainly a complication he didn't need. Her beauty was perhaps to blame. Even Ryan Jacobs, who was obviously very much in love with his wife, had been taken aback at first seeing Mae. John noticed the man's reaction, his eyes widening before he'd schooled his expression.

No doubt her exquisite flawless beauty was what affected him and why he felt the need to be always near her and keep track of her movements. That and her safety of course.

Someone as noticeable as Mae had to be kept safe; most men would take risks just to steal her away.

Chapter Nine

*J*OHN IS MARRIED. *John McClain is a lying bastard, who is married and has a child.* She didn't believe him when he later denied it. A sneer made her bare her teeth, and she cleared it away before Patty would notice it.

Once again, they were camped for the night after a day of riding in silence. Barely a word was shared between her and John. Truth be told, he had attempted to speak to her several times. However, each time she'd glared at him in response. He'd also apologized repeatedly for upsetting her, but had yet to explain why he'd not told her about his wife and child. What did it matter? She did not have any rights over the man. Yet for some reason, pushing away the anger at learning about the woman and child proved impossible.

When he'd kissed her back at the inn, she'd felt special as if it were they were the only two people in the world. Although there was no future for them, she at least expected over the time they'd become friends. He was special to her and she felt something extraordinary happened between them. Well at least it seemed so to her. Therefor it was now confirmed. She was a fool.

Something special bah! To John it was nothing more than a

kiss with just any woman. One thing living in a brothel taught her was men didn't care about such things as a wife and children waiting at home for them. Their only concern was taking care of their physical needs.

She chanced a look to where John and Ryan stood skinning some rabbits, only to look away quickly when John glanced her way.

"Ron tells me you two had a spat last night." Patty said, keeping her eyes on the potato she peeled. "It's only natural. I mean this journey is a hard one for someone just newly wed. You shouldn't stay angry with him Mae."

"There is just so much…" Mae wasn't sure what to say to the woman who'd become her friend. "It's just—I always considered John so stern and above reproach, yet the more I get to know him, the more I find he is…well sometimes he just makes me so mad." She finished not quite making sense.

"John does seem to be a hard man, yet he's gentle and caring with you. What did you fight about Mae?"

"A secret he kept from me. It's his right of course to keep things to himself, but I feel betrayed and hurt by it." Mae felt silly and mortified when a tear slipped down her cheek. What was wrong with her? "I am so confused right now."

She and Patty looked to the men, who'd stopped speaking and were now looking over at them with interest. "Come on Mae, let's go for a walk." Patty slipped her arm through Mae's and she guided her a ways until they came upon a fallen tree away from the campfire. Once they sat, Mae let out a breath. Patty was so easy to talk to, caring and gentle.

"Now tell me what's wrong. The truth." Patty looked her

in the eyes. "I know there is more to what's going on between you two than you're sharing, and it's fine Mae. It's your business. Just remember sometimes you have to trust God. He does things, brings people into your life for a reason."

"We are not married," Mae blurted and gasped at her words. Surprise did not register in Patty's expression.

"But you love him."

The statement so simply put, shocked Mae into the acknowledgement she'd loved John more than life itself for a long time, perhaps since the day they met. "Yes, I love him."

"And he loves you as well."

"Oh no, I don't think so," Mae protested. "He is just accompanying me to my father's ranch and then going on to…" She decided John's secret was his own, and it was better not to share. "Leave me." She finished with a shrug.

"I see the way he looks at you Mae," Patty covered Mae's hands with hers. "His face lightens when you appear, and he tracks your every movement. Hangs on every word you speak even when he's not looking at you directly."

"He's just attentive." Mae replied closing her eyes suddenly feeling drained. "I am just a burden to him."

"Why would you say that?"

Mae took a breath. She may as well lay it all out in plain sight; it was time to be honest. She'd never been anything but, and now she knew it was not in her nature to be otherwise.

"I met John one day about five years ago when I was returning from town. It was a beautiful day, and I decided to walk home. He came upon me. In his cavalry uniform on the big horse of his, he was every woman's dream. So handsome even with the ever-present stern expression of his, he stole my breath away. For the first time in my life, I was beyond words and in awe of a man. I hurried away from him because I didn't want him to know who I was and where I lived. I cringed when he dismounted and followed after me. When he caught my elbow and turned me to face him, I almost swooned. It's ridiculous of course, that he had an everlasting affect on me. Just to realize up close he was even better looking if that was possible was inconceivable to me. He smiled and introduced himself, touching my hand and giving a slight bow." Mae grinned at the memory. "I told him my name, and being he was not from town, it didn't mean anything to him. When he offered to walk me home, I tried to resist, telling him I preferred to walk home alone. However, he insisted. Along the way, we talked about our likes and dislikes, and about his work and what I'd purchased in town. We found out both our favorite color was blue and we both dislike cabbage. I memorized every word we spoke because I knew once he realized who I was, where I lived, he'd never treat me the same again." Mae braced herself keeping her eyes forward knowing once she divulged the truth the Jacobs would make an excuse and leave. She was not going to hide the truth.

"What do you mean by that Mae?" Patricia asked.

Mae looked away from her and continued. "The large white farmhouse where I lived came into view, and John attempted to steer me away, past it. I stopped at the gate and was not surprised to see the realization dawning in his eyes. 'I live here,' I told him and could see him physically recoil. John barely nodded when I thanked him for walking me home.

Instead of answering me, he shoved my parcel into my hands and looked at the house for a long while. Then he simply said goodbye."

Patty did not speak right away, her features neutral. She'd obviously figured out what Mae inferred because she didn't ask. Mae decided it was best to tell her just to make sure. "You see I lived in a brothel. My mother was a madam at the time. I still live there. After mother died, I took over the business. I am one of those shunned by society Patty. The only reason John agreed to accompany me on this trip is because the woman who raised me after my mother died pretty much forced his hand. He gave her his word."

She went to stand, and Patricia pulled her back. "I stand by what I said earlier. John McClain loves you Mae."

Mae was shocked at the gentleness in her friend's eyes and the lack of judgment or feeling any sense of Patty pulling away. She almost collapsed with gratefulness. "A man like John would never have me, Patty. I've accepted it a long time ago. He is bound by his upbringing, being from a well to do established family."

Her friend's arms went around her, and she relaxed into the woman's embrace. "We'll see about that," Patty huffed. "We'll just see about that," she repeated and soothed her rubbing her back.

And then Patricia asked her a question no one had thought to ask before. The question caught Mae by surprise. "Have you ever been a prostitute?"

And she answered honestly. "No, my mother made me promise I'd never sell my body, and Miss Lady has watched over me like a hawk to ensure I was never in a situation where it would come to be."

"Exactly what I thought." The woman gave her a wide smile. "It's obvious in the way you carry yourself around John and my husband although you put up a strong front."

"Will you tell your husband?"

"Don't worry Mae," Patty assured her. "I won't say a word about what we spoke of. Not even to Ryan."

Mae smiled at her new friend. "There shouldn't be any secrets between a married couple. You can tell him. Please, just not until after we arrive in Texas."

"I won't. And Mae it will be all right. I promise you this will work out." Patty crinkled her brow. "How is sleeping in the wagon working out?"

"We manage." Mae grumbled. "Back to back, as much space as possible between us."

"Ah," Patty giggled.

The women made their way back to the campfire, arms linked. Patty rolled her eyes at the men's attempts at stirring the potatoes. "I hope this meal agrees with Ryan. Last night he was making all kinds of music in his sleep."

Mae chuckled and clasped her hand over her mouth. She leaned into Patty's ear. "John snorts and mumbles. Snort, snort, mumble, mumble, snort." The women broke into peals of laughter, not stopping until both were wiping tears from their eyes.

When they noticed the men's gaping mouths and raised eyebrows, they began laughing again, leaning against each other until barely able to stand.

Chapter Ten

WHATEVER THE WOMEN found humorous made them laugh harder when they looked toward where he and Ryan sat. The peals of laughter continued while he watched Patricia and Mae stagger toward the campfire only to collapse onto the collapsed tree trunk.

Ryan shook his head. "Women! They cry one minute and laugh the next. Such emotional beautiful creatures are they not?"

With a smile, John nodded in agreement. "My sisters always kept me guessing. I have two, who seemed to hate and love each other from one moment to the next on a daily basis. My father always told me to just agree with them when they were in a state and leave from around them as quickly as possible."

"You're father is a wise man," Ryan replied eyeing the women who'd quieted and attempted to hide their smiles behind their hands. "Care to share what you find so funny?" Ryan asked, only to have the women begin laughing anew. "Yes, best to leave them be."

John watched Mae wipe tears away as she attempted once more to stop giggling. He'd never heard her laughter. It was a sweet, musical tone. And he wasn't aware she had such deep dimples in her cheeks. If he thought her beautiful before, now flushed and eyes sparkling, she was breathtaking. The stubborn woman caught him looking at her and pressed her lips together, instantly sobering. Patricia looked to him as well, and she continued to smile. "I'm sorry, we can't share it's something only women would find funny." Mae nodded in agreement, although she no longer smiled.

Ryan cleared his throat and motioned to John with his head. "Go on now. Spend some time with your wife, talk to her. Show her some affection." The man was intent on giving him advice on how to make amends with Mae. He'd informed him he was not demonstrative enough and did not show Mae sufficiently how he felt about her. John almost told Ron the truth just to put a stop to the marriage advice. Not deterred, the clergyman insisted on using his experience of ten years of marriage to help.

John stood and went to Mae. "How about we go for a short walk dear?" He asked, half expecting her refusal. Instead she looked to Patricia as if for permission or advice.

Ryan's wife pursed her lips and gave Mae a soft nudge. "Go on Mae. Listen to what your husband has to say."

Mae stood and attempted to move ahead. John took her hand in his and held her back to walk beside him. Her eyes were full of questions when they lifted to his. It wasn't surprising to him when she remained quiet. She was still angry.

When they moved out of earshot, he stopped and turned to her. "I'm going to kiss you Mae."

"What?" She looked over to where the Jacobs sat and back

to him. "Why?"

"Ryan is worried I'm neglecting my husbandly duties." Without preamble, not giving her an opportunity to protest, he leaned to her and pressed his lips against her. Her lips were soft against his. When he pulled back, she watched him with narrowed eyes. His heart quickened when her eyes flitted to his lips.

"I'm sorry Mae," he maintained eye contact with her. "I should have told you earlier about my situation. Explained it so there were no misunderstandings between us later. I was wrong not to be fully honest with you. Let's just get through these two weeks. We should be in Texas by then. By month's end, we will arrive where your father lives. Afterwards, we'll continue our separate ways."

"Stop apologizing John. We don't have to speak of it any longer," Mae told him flatly. "It doesn't matter. You didn't have to share anything with me. I have no right to be angry with you. Your private life is your own. And you are correct; after this week, we may never cross paths again, so let's forget about it."

The words should have made him feel better, but instead hollowness lodged in his chest and he couldn't think of an appropriate reply. She linked her hand through his arm. "Let's go back and eat. I'm tired and want to go to sleep early."

He didn't budge. "I'm glad you've become friends with Patricia Jacobs. Perhaps you two can remain friends in Texas."

Mae nodded. "Perhaps. They are not going to be living too far from my father's ranch. I haven't decided how much time I will remain there. I don't plan to stay long enough to make any friends. But I do feel a kinship with Patty and hope we will continue our friendship no matter if I return to Virginia."

He could only nod, not sure he could speak. That her words affected him so much surprised him. In a few days, they'd part ways and it should be a welcome relief. Instead he dreaded the day they went in separate directions. Her face was still flushed from laughing, a stunning sight, and he pulled her into his arms half expecting her to resist. With a soft sigh, she laid her cheek against his chest and slumped against him. It felt right, having her there and for a few moments they remained silent, the only sound the subtle breeze rustling the leaves overhead.

"If you need anything Mae, don't hesitate to send someone into town to find me. I will remain there for a few days until I take care of some business." His voice sounded husky in his ears, emotion filled.

She pulled back and arched a brow, the curve of her lips an enticing sight. "I won't John. You have to find your family and start your new life. My father is ill, and I don't foresee any problems. Just in case, if for whatever reason there is any kind of trouble, I will buy the stagecoach fare and return to Virginia."

They walked back to where the Jacobs sat, both sets of eyes locked to their hands which they held. Then Patricia gave them a wide smile and turned to Ryan who nodded approvingly at John. If they only knew. What he and Mae had just done was say good-bye.

"IS YOUR FATHER expecting you?" John asked Mae as they lay in the dark wagon the following night. "Is there someone there to greet you besides him? Ensure your safety?"

Mae sighed. "Yes, John. If I didn't know any better, I'd think you're worried about me with all the questions you're asking." She chuckled softly. "Miss Lady wrote them to tell them of my arrival. And yes, there is someone, a woman named Elma, who is taking care of him, his caretaker. Now let's sleep. Tomorrow will be a long day." Seeming more at ease now with his presence alongside her at night, she placed her hand on his shoulder. "Good night John."

He turned toward Mae and warm breath caressed his face. "I do worry about you. I care Mae."

The need to taste her became unbearable. John gave in, did not have the strength to resist the temptation. When he kissed her this time, it was impossible to stop. Yet reason left and all he knew was if he didn't hold her one last time to touch her and feel her softness against him, rest would not come on this night.

Mae must have felt the same way by the urgency by which she returned the kiss. The world could have gone up in flames and he would not have noticed. He wrapped his arms around her waist anchoring them against the too strong current.

Mae's hands slid over his shoulders to wrap around his neck and released a soft moan from deep in her throat. Any thought vacated, and all he knew was this woman represented everything he'd dreamed of since the day he'd first lay eyes on her. Mae felt exactly the way he'd known she would, fitting perfectly against him, her softness against his hardness, yielding and giving to his taking.

The heat in the small space became intense and their mouths refused to separate. The exploration of each other was far too enticing to draw back from.

The river of temptation began to pull him under until he couldn't breathe. John stopped kissing her, and closed his eyes holding Mae against him while he waiting for their breathing to stabilize. How could he ever let her go? This feeling with her was like no other he'd experienced. A loud sigh escaped him, and he began to trail kisses from her neck, to her throat, then back to her jawline only to stop when he tasted the salt of her tears on her face.

"Don't cry Mae, I'm sorry. I shouldn't have…" She placed fingers over his mouth stopping his words.

"Please don't say this was a mistake. I don't want to hear any remorse. Not tonight."

She released a heavy sigh and pushed her face into the crook of his neck. While holding her against him, he urged her face up to his. "It's not a mistake Mae, and I'm not sorry this kiss happened. I will never forget how you make me feel tonight. Thank you." He kissed her again this time a soft kiss, which he hoped, conveyed all he felt.

He continued to hold her, her head on his chest until she fell asleep, while he stared up into the darkness.

In her sleep, a shaky exhalation sounded, and he soothed Mae again. His heart pitched in his chest when she wrapped her hand around his arm as if ensuring he remained there with her.

He would for this night. He would stay forever, If only he

could get past knowing she'd slept with many faceless men, exchanging her enticing body for money. Not to mention, not only did he have the weight of having to find his child hanging over him, a feeling of foreboding he could not shake loomed over him. The pain in his leg was back, constant like before. For some reason, he felt as if his life would be affected by the injury, perhaps even killing him.

"YOU AND THE missus seem to be doing better," Ryan told John the next morning when they shared a cup of coffee. Dang if he didn't blush at the remark. John could only shake his head when the other man laughed at him. "We are."

"Good morning." Mae neared the coffee pot and poured a cup and then joined him on the log. Dressed in a simple blue muslin dress, with her hair in a braid down her back, she looked to be at ease, her face peaceful. She offered to refill their cups, and they held them out for her. For a moment, he allowed himself to believe she was in actuality his wife. His alluring partner.

When she blushed at his regard and smiled at him, his chest expanded with pride.

THE NEXT WEEK passed easily. Each night they'd developed an easy routine of discussing different experiences in their lives. This evening John lay on his back with an arm under his head he looked to her. "Who's taking care of your business while you're away?" He asked.

"Miss Lady and her daughter Lucinda will take good care of it. James helps with the books, so I'm not worried. Thankful actually to have three people I trust inherently." She began to explain the logistics of her business and astounded him speechless. She was an acute businesswoman who kept a close eye on expenses, balanced her ledgers routinely and ensured the needs of every person who worked for her was taken care of.

"I'm impressed," he admitted. "I'd need years of training before I could take over my father's business. You could walk in and take over immediately."

Mae chuckled. "I doubt it would take you years. Many months maybe."

They laughed, and John wondered if this was how a husband and wife spent their nights. He'd overheard the Jacobs' laughter on occasion, and it assured him to see that he and Mae too seemed to enjoy their hours alone.

The routine suited him more than he expected, and John had to admit he cherished their nights alone and the closeness they shared. The only difference in the passing days was he never kissed Mae again, not since the night when things had almost gone too far. Once one of them became groggy with sleep, they'd say goodnight and he'd roll to sleep to his side, his back to her.

DAYS LATER WHEN they crossed the Texas border, Mae become more withdrawn, and he gave her space. She needed to prepare herself for what was to come. She'd not mentioned her father again, which made him wonder if she would turn right around and return to Virginia once rested from her travels.

Dread loomed. Somehow he knew once separated from Mae, his life would change and not for the better.

Chapter Eleven

THE SIZE OF Hawkins Ranch on the outskirts of Hastings, Texas, her father's lands, was impressive. Mae lost count of how many fields filled with cows or planted with crops they rode by. The road toward an expansive farmhouse was lined with pecan trees with branches so heavy with nuts that they spilled over onto the well-packed dirty road. Her heart pounded inside her chest and she placed her hand over it. How would she be greeted?

Drained after a tearful goodbye with Patricia and Ryan, it took all her willpower not to beg John to turn the wagon around. Patty was optimistic, promising they'd visit soon, since they were less than a day's ride away, just on the other side of the small town of Hastings.

The amount of new sensations slamming into her in quick succession shocked Mae, and she wanted to buckle over and get sick. This had to be was the hardest day she'd ever experienced next to the one when her mother died.

John must have sensed her anxiety because he covered her hand with his and squeezed it gently. "It's a beautiful place. You'll be welcomed here and be just fine."

It was the first time since the night they'd kissed he'd

touched her. Since then, they'd slept back to back after only a few cursory statements. Of course it was for the best and she would miss him terribly.

Mae let out a shaky breath and pulled her hand from under his. "The sooner I face him the better. Then I can make a decision as to whether I will remain or not." Mae did not address his comment about the ranch. It was her father's property, and she had no desire to take it over.

As soon as the wagon pulled up to an expansive white-washed ranch home, the front door opened and a smiling middle-aged Hispanic woman followed by a large man who looked to be in his thirties came toward them. The man assisted Mae from the wagon. "Welcome Miss Hawkins. We're glad you made it safely. I'm Alan, your father's ranch hand." His friendly hazel eyes met hers briefly, and she found calmness in them.

"I better go help," Alan said after touching his hat and went to help John unload. John was already hauling her trunk toward the front porch. The ranch hand followed with her picnic basket and the other few things she's brought.

"You look like your father," the woman beamed at her and took her hands. "I am Elma." With a round face and bright brown eyes, Mae was further eased by the woman's smile.

Alan assisted unhitching Mae's horse and left with the beast towards where she assumed the barn was.

"Well that's it," John told her having returned to stand next to the wagon. He did not face her, but instead looked toward the porch where Alan was now pulling in her belongings through the door.

"This is John McClain who escorted me from Texas," Mae introduced him to Elma who began insisting he come inside for coffee and to rest.

John shook his head. "It's best if I get on my way, get to town before dark." His eyes met hers for a beat before he removed his hat and ran his fingers through his hair. "I'm not far. Send for me if you need anything." He went to the wagon and climbed onto the seat.

"John," Mae spoke to his back. He stopped but did not turn.

Seeming to understand they needed privacy, Elma scurried to the porch.

Mae walked around John and stood in front of him. He looked down at her, his impression impassive. "Thank you for escorting me," Mae began. "Please go see about your leg."

John nodded and remained without moving, seeming to wait for her to continue. She had so much to say, too many emotions churned inside that, if given free reign, she'd double over and falter. Instead she lifted her chin and looked him straight in the eye. "Goodbye John." She turned away and didn't stop until she stepped inside the house, closed the door behind her and slumping against it.

The darkened foyer was flanked on both sides with matching tall mahogany chests with gilded mirrors over them. Further down the hall, on the right, a large grandfather clock with a swinging pendulum counted off the seconds. Mae wanted nothing more at the moment than to fall into a bed and sleep. Cry from grief and exhaustion.

The sounds of the horse's hooves at a trot became softer

taking John further way from her with every passing moment. How was it possible? She missed him already.

Elma rounded the corner. "Oh Senorita, you are inside. Come let me show you to your room. I will draw you a warm bath. I expect you would like to get some rest." The woman continued chatting, her cheerful disposition helping keep Mae from allowing sadness to engulf her.

Pointing out rooms as she went, the woman guided Mae down a wide hallway. Since most of the doors were open, Mae peered in as they passed to find a large kitchen, a formal dining room, a study and two bedrooms. Elma stopped at the larger one. Her bags were already inside. "Senor Hawkins is asleep. He will not wake until morning. I gave him a sedative. His bedroom is on the opposite side of the house." Elma's lips curved to a soft smile. It did not reach her eyes and she fingered the hem of her loose blouse. "He will be happy to see you tomorrow. Today you bathe, eat and rest."

Elma pulled long curtains back, the setting sun lightened the large room and Mae took the opportunity to look around. The room was inviting with a large bed covered in off white linens, on one side side, a rustic tables. On the opposite wall from the bed, there was a large vanity, on it a mirror and brush set as well as a vase of fresh blue wildflowers. She went to the window and looked out. Across the vast expanse of land she spied some trees and flowering bushes. A garden.

"It's lovely, thank you Elma," Mae told the woman who watched her with expectation.

When Elma left with a promise of tea and a hot bath, Mae remained at the window. The view was indeed beautiful,

definitely a repose after days of hard travel. Her gaze traveled to
the plush bed, but she did not move toward it. No matter how
much she wanted to throw herself into the bed and find the
escape of slumber, it was not the time, not now.

LATER THAT NIGHT, Mae jerked awake and looked around
confused until she realized the space was a large bedroom and
not confined space of the wagon. It felt too large without
John's warmth next to her. Her hand slid across the bed to the
empty space; the sheets were cold under her palm.

He'd not told her how long he would remain in Hastings.
"A few days."

Were the woman and son there?

Was John laying next to her now? Was she happy to see
him?

No doubt anyone in a relationship with John would be
ecstatic to see him again and welcome the handsome man with
open arms. With an angry growl, she rolled away and yanked
the blankets over her shoulder.

"Elma! Come now!" The hoarse shouts permeated through
the fogginess of sleep and Mae instinctively knew it was her
father. "Elma!"

Not too far, a door opened and hurried footsteps followed.
Then nothing else. Mae considered if she should get up and see
what was needed, but decided it was best to wait. There was no
rush to face him and if he was having a hard time, she could
possibly upset him further.

Restless now, Mae sat up and scanned the dimly lit room.

She had to admit the house was elegantly decorated, no doubt the doing of her father's wife.

The time alone earlier had given her time to think. It was best if she spoke to her father, do what had to be done in quick order and remain only a few days before heading back to Virginia. This place was not for her.

First she'd insist her father leave anything meant for her to one of his legitimate children. If he expected to pay for his abandonment by gifting her the ranch, it was unnecessary.

A soft knock on the front door brought her out of her musing.

"Come in."

Elma stuck her head in and smiled. "Good morning senorita. Would you like some coffee or tea? Breakfast will be ready in an hour."

Mae shook her head. "You don't have to serve me. I can get it. Allow me to do for myself. It will give me something to do." She slid her feet off the bed. "As soon as I'm dressed, I'd like to come help you in the kitchen."

The woman's face fell, and she seemed to shrink back into the wall. "You don't plan to keep me here when you become mistress of the house?"

"Oh no!" Mae went to her and patted her shoulder awkwardly. "I just don't want to be an added burden to you right now. I imagine taking care of my father is a lot of work."

"Yes, it is," Elma acknowledged, "but I love to do what I can for Senor Hawkins. He has been kind to me and my family." The woman brightened and looked up at her. "Please relax Senorita Hawkins. I bring you coffee this morning, and after today, if you wish to take over some duties, let me know." With a quick smile, Elma left the room without waiting for Mae to respond.

Where were her father's children? Why was he alone with only Elma and Alan? Mae washed her face and dressed then sat to brush out her hair.

Elma returned with a tray.

"Will my father be at breakfast?"

"No, Senor Hawkins does not come to breakfast. He is too weak and cannot leave his bed any longer."

"Oh. I will go see him then. Is now a good time?" Mae asked.

Elma pressed her lips together. "I think it's better if you wait until after breakfast. I just gave him a dose of medication and he is resting."

"Where is his family? Why is he alone?"

"Senor Hawkins has no family senorita, just you. Senora Hawkins died five years ago. They had no children. The only family here is one nephew, Senora Mary's nephew, who helps Senor Joe with the horses. His name is Joshua. He is gone to deliver horses, should return in a day or two."

"Is Joshua close to my father?"

"Oh yes, very much so." Elma beamed. "He is a very good man. Senor Joshua has been helping Alan and the ranch hands. The poor man has been running things here for your father since he became ill and also working on his own ranch.

Interesting. "Why doesn't my father leave this ranch to Joshua then? It would make more sense than to give it to me. I don't have any experience nor am I even sure I will live here."

Elma frowned. "He has his reasons."

"Yes, I suppose I will find out after breakfast then." Mae sipped her coffee while Elma shook the linens and made her bed. Already she'd discovered several interesting things. But she didn't care to learn much more. This was only a visit, and once she met her father and talked with him, she'd let him know she planned to return to Virginia. This was about seeing her father and ensuring he realized she did not hold a grudge. The only questions would be out of curiosity, to know if she had any siblings and also perhaps find out the true reason he summoned her.

Yes, it was best she address her concerns with her father as soon as possible. Although she owed the man nothing, if he wanted to make amends before dying, there was no reason to deny him that.

Chapter Twelve

TODAY WAS NOT a good day to die. Neither was tomorrow actually. His entire body shook and his teeth chattered; yet he felt hot at the same time. John splashed cool water on his heated face from the basin in the hotel room. His stomach grumbled, the hunger almost unbearable. He should have asked about a room on the first floor. Just the thought of navigating the stairs to the first floor for breakfast made him feel sicker.

The second grumble motivated him, but his leg throbbing in response assured him that it would indeed be a torturous experience to descend. He looked at his reflection the mirror; his cheeks were hollowed, eyes glassy with purple circles underneath.

When was the last time he'd eaten? He pressed his lips together to keep from crying out when he moved back toward the bed and sat upon it, and a piercing ache throbbed deep into his leg muscle. In the two days since leaving Mae, his leg pain had worsened considerably. Once again the sense of dread enveloped him. Somehow he'd survive just long enough to find his child.

He said a prayer of thanks when a knock at the door sounded. "Please come in." His voice quivered slightly. A woman, who he recognized as the innkeeper's wife, slipped inside. She looked upon him and her mouth fell open, her eyebrows shooting high. It confirmed his belief. He must not look at all well.

"Would you like something to eat Mister McClain?" The woman asked. "We haven't seen you in a couple of days, so I thought it was best to check on you check and ensure all was well."

John sank further onto the bed, his shoulders leaning on the headboard. "Thank you ma'am, I'm obliged. I have been ill and not able to leave the room. Certainly would appreciate something to eat and perhaps some coffee."

"You seem to be running a fever. I can call Doctor Kennedy. You don't look well at all Mr. McClain." The rotund woman moved closer peering down at him with brows cinched together and placed the back of her hand against his jawline. "Mister McClain, you are very warm. I think you have a high fever. Let me send a boy to fetch the doctor right away."

"No, I thank you, but please don't call the doctor. I will go see him once I take care of some business. I'll be fine." He attempted to hide a shiver, yet she saw it by the thinning of her lips.

"Well all right, I'll see about getting you something to eat Mister McClain, but you should consider getting seen." She studied him with a scowl for a moment. "I'll bring you something for the fever."

The promise of food gave him energy. After she left, John got up and hobbled to the window to look down to the main street, which ran through the center of Hastings. On the street below, people moved about. A cart piled high with bales of hay passed, the driver reining back his horse when a man ran across the street waving at him to stop. The man caught up with the wagon, and after paying for it, he pulled a large bale of hay from the back of the wagon and tottered with it toward the stables. Two men on horseback pulled up at the saloon across from the hotel. Deep in conversation, they went inside. A trio of woman hurried past, their arms filled with parcels. From the looks of it, it was late in the morning.

Mae would like this town.

He caught sight of a woman exiting a doorway and leaned over the railing to wave at the women. *Dressmaker* was etched on the shingle over her head. Mae could live here with him. He shoved away from the window and almost collapsed from the pain the movement caused. "Damn it." With gritted teeth, he moved back to the bed. It was best he get Mae out of his head, stop thinking about her. Even if he survived this injury, there was no telling where he'd end up. Regardless of her lifestyle, Mae was used to a pampered secure life, which he could never provide, not if he continued to be sick or worse.

John shook his head at the direction of his thoughts, yet the picture of them together refused to dissipate.

IN THE LATE afternoon, through sheer willpower, John was able to get dressed and ride from town to the general area where he'd been told Carla and the outlaw lived.

Thanks to the medication the woman back at the hotel had

given him, John was able to ride without passing out from the pain. The fever had lessened, but the dizziness and aches, remained, although a bit dulled.

Several hours later, John grimaced while dismounting in a clearing, a short distance away from a shack with a lean-to tacked to its side. The drooping structure housed a thin horse. The wretched beast turned in his direction, its dull eyes taking him in.

John eyed the dilapidated cabin, attempting to determine if anyone was inside. How anyone could live in such deplorable conditions puzzled him. It seemed deserted, although with only one window, it was hard to see into the darkened interior.

With his eyes on the structure, John pulled Lasitor forward and maintained a good distance. Unsure if approaching was safe, he hesitated beside the horse. Just as he went to move closer, the fluttering at the edges of a tattered curtain told of someone watching him. John raised his hand toward the window, and the curtain fell back into place.

Moments later, the front door opened just enough for a thin tall women to squeeze through and close it firmly behind.

Carla? John remained where he stood, protected by the horse's rump. Once he ensured she was unarmed, he limped away from the horse the reins tight in his fist.

All sharp angles, with her bony arms swinging as she approached, John considered how strange it was he'd thought himself in love with her at one time. Now with a new perspective, he questioned those old feelings. Her harsh appearance coupled with the angry tightness of her lips changed what at one time was an attractive woman. The passing of years and her lifestyle had definitely changed her. Not been kind to her.

Dressed in dull brown skirts, she held the sturdy fabric up from the ground and neared him. Shrewd eyes met his and darted to his injured leg. "I thought you were dead. How did you find me?"

"Came close. I spoke to your sister. She told me you were here," he replied looking past her to the house. The curtain moved again, but he could not make out who looked out.

"Teresa could never keep her mouth shut. I shouldn't have said anything." Carla glanced over her shoulder toward the shack and back to him. "You should leave or this time you may not live John."

"I can't do that," John replied. "Is the child really mine?"

"Of course he is," Carla spat.

"He?" John swallowed at the news. "Look Carla, I didn't come all this way to argue with you. I want to meet my son and ensure he's taken care of. I promise not to interfere with your life. Be reasonable, I have a right to know my son. Allow me to see him."

"A right!" She backed up and put her hands up, fingers curled. "You never came back, never tried to see him for over three years. I sent word."

"To my parents, who didn't tell me after you refused to allow them to come and see about you nor did you accept their invitation to live with them." She rolled her eyes and John blew out a breath to keep from losing his temper with her. "I was away, assigned to a remote location. There was no way for me to come and see about you. When I did come, I got shot."

"It doesn't matter anymore. I've made a life for myself and

Wesley. We don't need you. I tried to keep my husband from shooting you. You startled him."

Wesley. He'd not heard much more than that. John held back from rushing past her and going into the dwelling. He'd come so close, and the possibility of meeting his child made it hard to now shove the woman out of his way and see if she spoke the truth. "Let's just cease this nonsense. Let me meet my boy and I'll be on my way."

Carla seemed to soften until once again she looked toward the house. "Look, please just go John. My—my husband will shoot you if he finds you here. You're lucky he's out back hunting right now."

"I want to see my son." He repeated not moving.

Nervous hands twisted the fabric of her skirts. "What for? We're not staying here long anyhow."

"I'm not going to stop coming after you until I see him." John stated not sure how he'd manage to keep his word, yet he would.

"You calling the law on him?" She was obviously not speaking of Wesley.

"No, I don't plan to."

She took a step away. John touched her arm, stopping the woman from leaving, and her eyes snapped to his hand. "Look, I'm staying in the hotel in town. Can you bring him? I won't bother you afterwards. I promise you."

"Maybe…yeah, I suppose I can do that." She hesitated for a moment, as if meaning to say something else and then continued to walk to the house her shoulder's stiff.

Without any choice, he returned to town.

"MISTER MCCLAIN," THE doctor tapped at the syringe and leaned in to inject him in the thigh. "I'm afraid it can't be put off much longer. You must make a decision very soon. If not, you will die. If it were up to me, I'd take care of it today."

"You don't mince words, do you Doc?" John winced at the medicine pushing into his muscle. "There is something I must take care of. It should only be a matter of days. And please call me John."

The doctor met his gaze with a scowl. "It's your life, your decision. It may already be too late. I will come back and see you tomorrow." He uncapped a bottle and held up a dropper. "Lift your tongue."

John swallowed the bitter medication. "I'll have a decision to you tomorrow then. Can I ride today?"

"You shouldn't have ridden as much as you already have. If you can walk down the stairs, which I doubt, then you can ride." The doctor smiled, his eyes full of kindness. "John, be reasonable, you can barely sit. I'll see you tomorrow."

He remained in bed and closed his eyes, hearing the doctor's footsteps move toward the doorway. "Thanks doc."

The door closed and opened again, followed by more shuffling. It didn't matter to him at this point who entered. He kept his eyes closed while attempting to absorb the fact that in a day or two his life would be altered forever.

"John." Carla's voice penetrated the fogginess the medication brought.

His eyes flew open, and he struggled to sit, biting back the searing pain shooting up to his hip. Carla stood beside the door. Just behind her a child peered at him, his body hidden by her skirts.

"I didn't expect you would really come." John pulled the blankets over his bare legs and waited for her to speak.

"After your visit yesterday, my husband and I had a long discussion. We decided our life was hard enough without a child along. We have plans, big plans. Like going further west…well, Bart wants a try at the gold you know?" She wringed her hands and wiped them on her skirt. "You see it's for the best if Wesley lives with you. Just don't call the law on us."

John looked to the boy who studied him with concentration far too intense for such a young child. "What are you saying Carla?"

"You're his father; you can raise him." She pulled the boy around to her front. Dark haired with serious eyes, the three year old held a small bundle and looked up at his mother with expectancy.

Oddly, Carla didn't look at the child, her unfocused eyes on him instead. "Wesley, this is your father. Stay and be a good boy." Chin jacked up, Carla rounded the boy and rushed out, the door closing firmly behind her.

The boy's bottom lip quivered, and John braced himself for the wailing that would surely follow. Instead the child took a shaky breath, scratched at his head and sat on the floor. With his elbow on his leg and chin cupped in his hand, the child sighed again. "I hungry." The boy's serious eyes shifted to him.

"Great," John groaned and looked up at the ceiling. "What am I going to do now?"

Chapter Thirteen

"HELLO DAUGHTER," THE voice sounded familiar, but Mae could barely make out the man's features in the darkened room.

"Would you like me to open the curtains?" She asked, not sure what to do and not comfortable enough to go near him yet.

"Sunlight would be most welcome," he replied and began to cough, his entire body shaking. She waited by the window until he finally took a deep breath and stopped. Her father motioned to a chair across from the bed.

Finally Mae was able to get a good look at him and studied the ailing man who was propped up in bed, surrounded by pillows, while watched her in return.

Elma hustled in with a cup of steaming liquid and placed it in on a tray that she placed over his legs.

Mae watched her father bring a cup to his lips with shaky hands and suppressed the need to offer help. He barely resembled the man she remembered from childhood. Although still a large man, he was gaunt and his skin was yellowed with sickness. The mostly gray, unkempt hair and drooping jowls overwhelmed what had once been a handsome face. Yet, his still clear intelligent green eyes commanded attention. They were the exact shade as hers.

When Joe Hawkins brought the cup back down to the saucer, he turned his attention back to her and began to speak without preamble, as if he'd been waiting for the opportunity to impart the information before it was too late. "The ranch is self-sufficient; the gardens produce potatoes, carrots, cabbage and other vegetables. Elma can fill you in on all the details. Our meat comes from the cattle, pigs and chickens. Of course milk and eggs are also plentiful, so there is no need of anything from town other than basic grains, fabric and such." He closed his eyes and groaned. "This damn pain won't go away. Would you please hand me the laudanum?"

She did as he asked and watched him place two drops into his tea. "If you are tired, we can continue this some other time…"

"I'm afraid I don't have the luxury of time. I don't have much left," his shrewd eyes took her in. "And don't think about arguing with me or saying you won't remain here young lady. This land is your birthright and your due. I owe you much more than I am giving you. What I owe you cannot be paid with land and money. Hate leaving you with all the work that comes with this place. Thankfully Alan Murphy, who you've met, is a good ranch hand. He's not been here long. However, in the short time he has shown himself to be a capable rancher. I suspect Joshua, my wife's nephew, will help you in spite of all the work he already has over at his place. He also is a good man."

Mae nodded, not wanting to upset him. The conversation

about who'd get the property would be between her and Joshua. For now, she'd remain quiet about it to placate the ill man.

"You don't favor your mother much." The statement took her by surprise. "She was very attractive, but you are stunning my dear. Quiet too, she wasn't much for biting her tongue." He smiled at her.

"On most occasions neither am I." Mae couldn't help but smile back at him. "I believe I favor you physically; however am more of her temperament."

"Lord I hope not," he began to cough and waved her away with ill concealed impatience when she went to move closer. "I'm dying Mae, slapping my back only irritates me."

"Don't say that…"

"It's the truth. I've come to terms with it. I just ask you sit with me and let me get to know you. Tell you as much as I can about myself and your inheritance." Mae clenched her teeth; he didn't have a right to ask anything of her. Her father chuckled. "You're probably thinking I'm lucky you even came." He was right of course. "And you're right about that. I was proud and stupid. When your mother told me she was expecting, it was right after I'd become engaged to Mary. My fiancée was a good woman. And she came from a respectable, wealthy family. At first I planned to return here to Texas and break off the engagement. Then I became terrified. And well too proud to admit to her family and mine I'd been unfaithful to Mary and fathered a child out of wedlock. At twenty-eight, I should have known better. Instead of cowering, I should have been a man and not succumbed to pride. I admit her money was also a factor." Well his statement cinched it; he was her father. Honest to the point of crassness.

He'd been the same age as she was now. She could relate to pride, but greed, was something she didn't understand. "So now you get this large ranch and it is prosperous, so something came of my cowardly act I suppose."

His chuckle was without mirth. "The sad thing is, I bought it and prospered this ranch without any monetary help from Mary or her family. After meeting you, guilt followed me, a heavy burden I could not lay down. I threw myself into work and prospering this land." He shook his head. "I will admit to you I fell in love with your mother the instant I met her, and I wish I'd never abandoned her. It was the hardest thing I've ever done."

Mae blinked at his confession. If only her mother had known. Perhaps she did; they had both loved each other, and the ending was tragic. On some level she could relate to it.

"Mary and I never had much of a marriage. Through the years, she was a good wife to me." Her father continued.

"What happened to her?" Mae asked.

Her father looked past her to a dresser along the wall. Mae followed his line of sight to see a portrait of a young dark-haired woman dressed in a flowing gown. With a hand on her lap and another on the arm of a chair, she looked into the distance, her face solemn except for a slight lift at one side of her mouth. "Mary died of a pneumonia; she was always frail."

"I'm sorry."

"Yes well, I am too. I never made her happy. Sometimes I wondered if she grieved for another, a lost love or heartbreaking romantic interest. She never said anything. At times however, her melancholy was so heavy, it weighed down those around her." Again he closed his eyes, this time his breathing became labored.

Mae studied the woman in the picture, the eyes told a story of loss and sadness. So much like her mother's. "I should let you rest."

"Come visit me after supper daughter. I would like to speak of the accounts. Bring the ledgers with you. Elma knows where they are kept." His eyes closed and his rasping pants slowed.

Making her way to the kitchen, Mae stopped at the doorway into the large room to the right of the entryway. A huge fireplace flanked by twin leather chairs, each with a wooden footstool faced another pair of wooden chairs with overstuffed cushions. Over the fireplace a rustic mantle, over it a large landscape painting of what looked to be the surrounding lands. The curtains framing the windows were long and cream colored, the thick fabric capable of keeping light out and heat in.

She moved inside running her hand along the back of one of the chairs. Her eyes took in the room, lighting on a large porcelain vase. It was painted with an intricate design of a floral bouquet that took her breath away. She traced it with a fingertip. *Could I live here?*

"Hello cousin," at the masculine voice Mae gasped and thrust the vase forward. The vessel tottered, and she grabbed it with both hands to steady it.

A stocky sandy brown haired man who looked to be about thirty stepped toward her. "I'm sorry. I thought you heard me walk in." He held his hand out. "I'm Joshua, and you must be Mae."

Mae shook his hand. "Hello Joshua, I've heard good things about you. I just left my father's room, I suppose I was deep in thought and didn't hear you approach."

Joshua nodded. "How is he?"

"Elma says he seems better. To me he looks frail and in a lot of pain."

"Uncle Joe has been hanging in there waiting for you to return. He's a strong old man." Sorrow etched on his face when Joshua's brown eyes searched hers. "I don't expect you'll believe me, but he cares for you deeply."

She bit back an irate retort; it wouldn't do any good to argue with people who obviously held her father in high regard. "I want to talk to you about the ranch. It doesn't strike me as fair for it to be given to me and not you. It's obvious my father cares for you, and you've been working the land. Not to mention, you've been here all along to help."

Joshua smiled. "Aunt Mary left me her lands. They neighbor Hawkins' lands on the east side and rivals them in size. A couple hundred acres of prime, rich land is all mine." He gave her an easy smile and she found it easy to relax with him. "I appreciate it Mae, but I don't need what by all rights belongs to you."

"I—I don't know anything about ranching," Mae stuttered. "I'm not even sure wish to remain in Texas."

"Well, you'll make the right decision when the time comes. I'll help you hire another good ranch hand to help Alan if need be. I've been lending a hand since Uncle Joe took ill. To continue for much longer is too much for me to do alone with only Alan."

"I see." Mae sunk into the nearest chair. "I appreciate your honesty. You could have just taken the ranch and sold it or something."

"Now that would not be right." Joshua gave her a patient look, which made her feel childish. "It's all right to be scared Mae, but the land out there." He pointed out the window. "Well Mae, it's your birthright and if you're meant to stay, it will call to you to do so." He took a breath. "Well, I better go see the old man. Nice meeting you."

Mae listened to Joshua's footsteps until they became faint. Would she remain in Texas? Maybe her future was here. The only truth right now was she just missed John. It was the only truth. This was not what she expected at all. No, she thought at the most she'd remain two weeks, speak to her father and book a passage on the stagecoach back to Virginia. Now she wasn't sure if she could leave, at least not until she figured out what to do with the land. Her father was on the brink of death, the glaze in his eyes, the dullness, being telltale signs of an imminent end.

Gray eyes formed in her mind, followed by John's face and then the distinct line of his straight nose, and smooth jawline. The depth of his voice when he'd moaned while kissing her, echoed in her mind. Mae squeezed her eyes tight needing to keep the vision longer. Surely he didn't think of her. No, he was reunited with his family and starting a new life. At the thought of him kissing another woman, a knot formed in her throat and she struggled to swallow. "No."

"Senorita, dinner is ready." Elma interrupted her thoughts. "Would you like it brought here?"

Mae straightened and lifted her hand to her hair to smooth it from her face before turning to the woman. "I would appreciate it. Thank you, Elma. And can you tell me where the ledgers are please? Father wants to review them with me after I eat so I'd like to look them over."

Elma went to a cabinet to the right of the door and opened a drawer. From it she pulled two large ledgers and brought them to Mae. "This one is for household expenses," she handed it to her. "And this one is where the Senor Hawkins keeps track of all the other ranching expenses and incoming money."

AFTER DINNER, MAE went to see her father to find him fast asleep. She stood over him for a few moments and watched his chest rise and fall, his breathing labored. Sadness filled her at the realization she'd never get to know him. At least the hatred and anger she expected didn't fill her. Holding the ledgers in her lap, Mae sat in a chair to continue watch over him. When he woke, they would discuss the accounts. Although they were well kept and organized, she doubted it would take very long for him to be satisfied she had the gist of what needed to be done to keep them straight.

The thud of one of the ledgers slipping off her lap and hitting the floor woke her. Her father continued on deep in slumber, and Mae rose to go and do the same. When she bent to collect the book off the floor, she noticed the corner of a picture frame which had been tucked or fallen under the nightstand. She picked it up and was astonished. It was picture of her mother and herself at about five or six.

The last time he'd visited perhaps? What a tragic story it turned out for all those involved. Her father succumbed to the pressures of a well to do family, and her mother was ostracized for becoming pregnant out of wedlock. Thankfully, her family from Northern Virginia gave her the house in Widow's Peak. Then they'd promptly all but disowned her. Although her father married, neither got their happily-ever-after.

Chapter Fourteen

TWO DAYS AFTER Carla had left Wesley in his care, the ever-present fever became worse, and John lost hope he'd be able to care for the child. Death was now something he feared. The last thing he wanted for his son was to be abandoned and alone in a strange town with no one to care for him.

John shook so hard his teeth chattered, yet he managed to guide the horse down the winding road on Hawkins lands to the main house. *Lord, don't let her be gone, not yet.* He repeated the prayer he'd been chanting in his mind over and over again. Mae had told him she didn't plan to stay long, yet he hoped she'd decided to remain for while longer. Surely she'd not left so soon, needing time to recover from the travel here.

Wesley sat next to him, silent, holding his precious bundle. His eyes shifted up to John's face every few minutes as if to assure he'd not passed out. He had wondered about it himself several times during the six hours it took to get there. Although the boy was no more than three, he had a mature calmness about him. John took strength from it, and it steadied him.

The large ranch house finally came into view, and John breathed a sigh of relief. "See the house Wes? We're going there."

"House," Wesley repeated his eyes wide. "Big."

"Yes, it's very big," John replied and repeated the prayer. Mae had to be there. Otherwise, his options were to find a place to live with Wesley and somehow hire someone to help care for him while he recovered, if it was even meant to happen. He wasn't sure he could do it, not with the way the raging fevers and pain continued to assault.

The door opened and the short Hispanic woman he'd met last time came outside just as he pulled the wagon to a stop in front of the large ranch home. Her eyes went from him to Wesley and back. "I remember you. You are Senorita Mae's friend. Come inside." She rounded the cart to Wesley's side and held her hands up to the boy. "Well hello boy, come here let me help you down." John watched as his son held his arms out seeming to accept the woman as a friend.

The woman met his gaze over the child's head, concern evident at seeing the sheen of perspiration on his face. "Come inside Senor, I have some fresh lemonade."

John's mouth watered at the thought and he climbed down not able to suppress the groan at the piercing pain. With each step, he wanted to crumble to the floor. "Thank you Ma'am. Is Mae here?"

The woman nodded, and relief flooded him so hard his legs almost buckled. "Si, she is here. My name is Elma," she told Wesley who regarded her with interest. "Come. Inside. Once I serve you a cold drink, I will let senorita Mae know you are here." The woman made her way inside with Wesley in her arms as John followed barely able to keep his balance.

The boy watched him over Elma's shoulder, and without

blinking he tracked John's movements. A pang of guilt built in John's chest at how unsteady his son's life was. John did not look away; his son needed reassurance from him right now.

Once he'd limped through the entryway into the house, John placed a small bag with a change of clothes just inside the doorway in the dimly lit hallway and forced himself to keep up with the woman and his son as they made their way to where he assumed was the kitchen. Pulses throbbed up his leg with each step until his breathing became so labored he had to stop and lean against the wall.

Elma materialized and grabbed his arm, urging him forward. "Senor, you are not well at all. Doctor Kennedy will be here later to see Senor Hawkins, and I will ask him to see you."

"Good, yeah…I planned to see the doctor in a day or two. Just need to rest a bit."

The woman did not reply, and by the set of her lips pressed together into a tight line, John knew she didn't agree. He was already going to ask too much of them, so the last thing he needed to burden them with was his illness.

THE SOUND OF voices traveled down the hallway, Elma and a muffled masculine voice. From the tone of the conversation, it was someone the woman knew. If it were someone from town, then hopefully they'd leave right away and were there only to see Elma. She was not in the mood for visitors. Most of the night her father had moaned in pain, and she'd remained by his bedside dolling out regular quantities of medication. Exhaustion did not begin to cover how she felt at the moment.

Even the thought of going to the kitchen to get some tea before lying down for a few minutes would be a hardship for her at this point.

Mae arranged the blankets across her father's chest. He'd barely spoken today, his eyes continuingly closing and his breathing became more and more labored as time progressed. She'd been hesitant to wake Elma up and send someone to fetch the doctor. Thankfully when the woman finally came to check on him the next morning, he seemed better. Doctor Kennedy was due to come any minute, so they'd wait. She looked to the doorway; maybe the male who'd arrived was the doctor, as it was possible he decided to arrive earlier.

Mae leaned closer to the slumbering man, and placed her hand on his forehead. He felt cool to the touch, no fever.

A tremor shook him and his eyes opened. "You are still here." The weak statement scared more than reassured her. "Don't worry 'bout me. I'm going to die a happy man knowing you are where you deserve to be." His eyes closed again. A soft moan followed by tremors began again. She pulled on his chin to open his mouth and dispensed two drops of medication.

Minutes passed, and the moaning continued. This was troublesome. Mae scrambled from the room. "Elma! Come at once." She rushed down the hallway to the kitchen. He couldn't die. Not yet. Suddenly, she was not ready to let him go.

"Senorita, what is it?" Elma stopped her just as she got to the kitchen doorway. "Is the Senor in a bad way?"

"Y—yes…" Mae stuttered only to stop speaking at seeing a pale John sitting at the kitchen table. He had a glass of lemonade in front of him, his hand wrapped around it.

When he went to stand, Elma went back to where he was and pushed him back down with a firm hand on his shoulder. "You should remain seated Senor McClain."

"What's wrong John?" Mae went to him brushing hair away from her face with the back of her hand distracted by the new matter at hand. "Are you sick?"

Despite his sallow skin and dark circled eyes coupled with the sheen of sweat on his face John's voice was strong. "I've had better days. I need to speak to you." His gaze swept to the boy and warmed. "My son needs a place to stay while I recover."

"Of course," Mae replied, distracted by the thumping of her heart at John's presence. She looked back to Elma. "Please send someone to fetch Doctor Kennedy; my father needs him now." She turned an accessing eye to John. "And he can see John while he's here too." Elma rushed to the back door and exited.

"You will stay here for a few days. You don't look well enough to travel right now."

John opened his mouth as if to argue but stopped when she tapped her foot and nodded, "I'd appreciate it."

Not sure what to do, Mae took a breath. "I will get a bedroom ready for you." Her eyes swept to the other side of the table, and she noticed a small child who sat opposite John. He'd not moved since she'd entered, so she'd missed him being there. What was she thinking? Of course it was John's child. He'd mentioned needing the boy to stay. She swung back to John. "Did his mother come with you?"

"No, just us two."

She made her way toward the child. "My name is Mae." Her attempt at a smile failed.

Exact replicas of John's serious eyes looked back at her. The boy seemed at ease around strangers. "Hello."

"His name is Wesley," John told her. "My son."

"It's more than obvious since he's your spitting image." Mae patted the boy's head and looked at John who stared at the boy as if noticing the resemblance for the first time.

"He's got your eyes, dark hair and seems to have your personality as well."

He gave her a questioning look.

Elma came back inside. "Alan is gone to fetch Doctor Kennedy. I will go see about Senor Hawkins."

"No," Mae stopped her. "I will go back. Please see about Mister McClain and Wesley." She was not ready be alone with John, didn't want to know why he was there with only his son. Not today. Thankfully, he did not try to stop her.

She went back to her father's bedroom to wait for the doctor to arrive but could not sit still. Twice she went to the door and started to leave, turned away and paced back to the window. Maybe she should go and talk to John, if he planned to leave the child with her. Where was the boy's mother?

John's wagon remained in the front of the house. Alan appeared and drove it away to the back where the stables were.

Why was John here? Why did he come alone with only the child? It was obvious he was very ill. Her face softened at recalling the small child. He was adorable; no doubt a replica of what John had looked like as a babe. Did John leave the boy's mother? Was it possible? No, perhaps, she was away, and John needed help caring for the boy. Wesley. Yes that was his name. John needed help with Wesley since he was not feeling well.

HER HEAD FALLING forward snapped Mae awake at Doctor Kennedy's voice just outside the doorway. The opening of the door made her jump to her feet and move toward it. Elma stood with him, a grim expression on her face. The doctor moved past Mae into the room and she would have followed him except for Elma taking her arm.

"Allow Doctor Kennedy to see after your father. Come have a cup of tea in the kitchen with me. You look exhausted."

She turned to look at the man in the bed, a virtual stranger yet she could not stop the sorrow from engulfing her. "All right, yes." Mae permitted Elma to steer her toward the kitchen.

They drank tea in silence for a few minutes, Elma watched her closely. "You have a good heart Senorita. You care for your father even though you never got to know him well." Elma shook her head at her shrug. "He loves you. A day rarely passed that he didn't mention you."

Mae heaved a sigh. "I don't know what I feel. Perhaps it's just that I don't like to see anyone suffer… Speaking of which, where are John and his son?"

"Senor McClain went to lie down, and the child is asleep as well. I gave him something for the fever," Elma replied. "He said he felt bad asking you to look after the boy for him until he recovers."

"Oh," Mae replied, not sure what to think. "Did he say

what was wrong?"

"I think he is very ill. Do you not have any idea?"

"No…well, his leg is injured. He was shot." Mae wondered if perhaps it had become infected again. "Doctor Kennedy should see about him once he finishes with father."

As if prompted, the doctor called for them, and both went to the master bedroom. "I'm sorry." His somber eyes met hers and then Elma's. "Your father has passed away Miss Mae," the doctor turned to the bed. "I'll give you some time with him."

Elma linked her arm through Mae's, her brow pinched. The woman no doubt was suffering even more than she. After all, she'd lived there for years, had known her father well. Mae patted the woman's hand, and Elma looked up her eyes filled with tears.

"Doctor, please wait." Mae went to him and told him about John. She went down the hall to the bedroom next to her and opened the door. Both John and Wesley were asleep, with the boy snuggled next to John's much larger body. Mae smiled at the sight and captured it in her mind. She picked up the boy, and John woke.

"I'll leave you to see about him doctor." Mae walked out with the sleeping child in her arms and placed him in her bed then went back to find Elma.

JOSHUA WALKED INTO the front room an hour later. He went directly to her father's bedroom and came back only a few minutes later ashen. "Uncle Joe wanted to be buried over in the east field next to Aunt Mary. I'll take care of it." Joshua fidgeted with his hat and looked to Mae. "If there's anything you need, I'm right next door."

What could she possibly need? Her life, if she chose to remain in Texas, was set. No money problems, an honest existence. And Virginia, although not the best of circumstances, was a familiar comfortable place.

"We can discuss later if anything it all rightly belongs to you." Mae replied.

Joshua walked over and placed his hand on her shoulder. "Don't think or say anything else on the matter. I am happy and don't begrudge you this house or the land. Like I said before, Aunt Mary and Uncle Joe took very good care of me. They were the best parents anyone could wish for. Raised me, being mine died when I was fourteen."

When Joshua left, Mae closed her eyes and immersed herself in the total silence of the moment. Elma was making arrangements for the wake, and Doctor Kennedy was still with John.

She let out a breath and opened her eyes at the sound of soft footsteps. Wesley stood at the doorway, his dirty bundle against his chest. "Momma?"

Mae went to him and scooped him up as he began to cry. "No baby, don't cry, please don't cry. I don't know where your momma is, and I am afraid if you keep crying I'm going to have to cry with you."

The little boy clung to her, his little body shaking as he sobbed and took shaky breaths in between. Mae began to him rock back and forth while rubbing his back. When Wesley continued to cry, she began to sing. It was an old song Miss

Lady would sing to her when she cried for her mother.

"*Sweet and low, sweet and low Wind of the Western Sea*"

"*Blow, blow, breathe and blow Wind of the Western Sea*"

"*Over the rolling waters, blow, Come from the dying moon and blow…*"

Finally after little Wesley stopped crying and laid his head on her shoulder, he took another shaky breath. "Momma," he whispered.

Mae cradled him against her until his little body went limp and the bundle fell to the floor with a soft thump. She bent to pick up the pitiful parcel and returned to her bedroom, thankful the sleeping child could not see her tears. "Oh darling where is your mother?" She kissed his soft hair and laid him in her bed. He stirred a bit, but thankfully continued to sleep.

"Miss Hawkins?" Doctor Kennedy peered in from the doorway. "I must speak to you. It's urgent."

After a quick wipe at her cheeks with the back of her hands, she followed the doctor to the kitchen. When he hesitated, she poured him a cup of coffee he readily accepted. Lines of fatigue stretched across his brow, the man sat and took a couple swallows of the hot liquid. "I'm afraid I have to lay the burden on you of making a very difficult decision for John."

Mae sunk into the nearest chair. "I'm exhausted Doctor Kennedy. I am not sure I have any strength left." She looked to the back door desperately wishing someone would enter and take control of the situation that was about to get much worse. When no one did, Mae sighed and met the doctor's eyes. "Is John going to die too?"

"No Miss Hawkins, not if I amputate his leg today."

Chapter Fifteen

C LOUDS COVERED THE sun, and the day turned gray. Fitting, Alan thought and leaned against the rail. He looked toward the interior of the ranch house. All the windows had light pouring out from them. He lit a cigarette and inhaled the sweet tobacco deeply before releasing the smoke. Things were chaotic inside, death did that, made people spur into action. Something he was quite familiar with.

Without thought he rubbed the center of his chest. The familiar pang did not lessen. Footsteps neared, and Joshua came to lean against the fence beside him. "Could use a hand digging the grave."

"Yeah, I figured as much, got the shovels," Alan said and motioned with his head to the tools next to him. "The old man will be put to rest right. He deserves it."

"Can I have one?" Joshua motioned to his hand rolled. They remained quiet for a few minutes before Joshua spoke. "You're going to have to hire more help, will need more ranch hands before the harvest."

"Just tell me where to go. I'll take care of it."

"Mae doesn't know anything about ranching; however she's smart. I can tell it in her eyes. She's a business woman back in

Virginia." Joshua told him.

Alan nodded, without speaking.

"Don't know about a woman living alone here. Not married and all." Joshua mumbled.

"You thinking about offering?" Alan said, only to shrug when Joshua's widened eyes met his. "She's a beauty."

"Yeah—yeah she is, seems to me she's got something going with that man, the one who escorted her from Virginia. He's here now, came with a child." Joshua went for the shovels. Talk time over. The man grabbed a shovel and walked away. When Alan went to follow the back door of the house opened.

Elma hurried out and headed for him. The sorrow etched on her face made Alan look away past her shoulder to the tree line, the reminder of days past pounding at his temples.

"Senor Alan, can you please go to town and get the pastor to come for the burial tomorrow?" The woman clutched a handkerchief and twisted it until Alan thought it might tear in half.

"Yes, I'll go as soon as I finish helping Joshua with the grave." He threw the last of the hand rolled down and ground it into the dirt with his boot. "Don't worry about anything Elma. You've got my help for anything you need."

"Thank you Senor Alan." Elma dabbed fresh tears that slid down her cheeks and looked toward Joshua who was already headed to the tree where they were digging. "You are a good man."

A good man. Alan stared at the ground, and he wondered if anything was left in him which could be called good. Empty, hollow, desolate, yeah those fit a lot better.

Chapter Sixteen

J OHN'S HEARTBREAKING SCREAMS pierced straight into her soul, and Mae lost all ability to control her reaction. She jumped from a chair in the front room and raced down the short hallway toward the bedroom where she'd been barred from entering just minutes earlier.

Finding the door locked, she pounded on it with her fists and shouted her shrieks mixing along with John's. Each peal of sound from the other side of the doorway echoed the terror clawing through her entire being.

"Please don't! I've changed my mind! Don't do it." Why did they not answer? Joshua, Elma and the doctor were in there; surely one of them heard her.

When her cries continued unanswered, Mae kicked at the door and tried to twist the doorknob, neither gave way. "Doctor Kennedy, please don't do it. I made a mistake." Her words became mere gasps as she slid down to the floor and sobbed into her hands. Oh God, he's going to hate me. He will never forgive me for this. What have I done?

Another scream pierced the air, and she slammed her fist against the door again. When it too went unanswered, Mae clawed at the door. "Please open the door, don't do this." God she had no right to make such a decision for John. Why had she not insisted they wait another day, another few hours to see if he came to? He'd passed out from the fever, but he'd made it through before, surely he would have this time.

Bloody trails of where her fingernails cut into the wood did little to deter her. She began to pound again. Finally the door opened, and she struggled to get to her feet. Unfortunately she was too drained and her legs refused to budge. "Don't do it, please." She whispered. "Please."

Strong arms slid around her and pulled her to her feet.

"Mae, you're not helping things," Joshua's calm voice washed over her, and she looked up with desperation.

"Oh God Joshua, please help me. Go back inside and make the doctor stop." Mae grabbed his shirt and shook him, her fingers leaving bloody imprints. "They must not do this."

"It's done. The doctor is stitching him up now. John's passed out is why he's quiet. The poor man remained conscious the entire time."

Mae began to sob uncontrollably, and Joshua pulled her against him. "Shush now Mae, it has to be done. Doc said he would've died for sure, the infection was so bad."

"Oh my God," her knees gave out, and Mae would have fallen to the floor, if not for Joshua who scooped her up and carried the weeping woman to the bedroom. It felt as if she was going to pass out as well as everything went out of focus; she barely felt Joshua lay her on the bed.

"Now stay here and try to calm down. I'll get you some whiskey. Doc don't need any more distractions right now." Joshua walked out.

What would John do now? This had to be the worst day of her life. She turned her face into the pillow and began to scream into it until her throat was raw, and then she kept on.

EXHAUSTION FILLED HER days. Seven days, an entire week had passed since John lost his leg, and each day had become a replica of the last. It was dusk and Mae sat with Wesley. She read to him while the child attempted to remain awake snapping his eyes open when they began to close. Her own eyes felt heavy at the moment as well.

If it weren't for having to check on John's wound and clean it again, she would allow sleep to come. When the boy's eyes finally remained closed, she slipped from the bedroom where he slept and made her way to where John was.

JOHN'S SOFT BREATHING was the only sound in the room until Mae poured the hot water into a clean basin and dipped white sterilized cloths into it.

With careful hands, she pushed the light blanket up to his thigh and lifted the leg thankful she could do this now without eliciting moans from him. The sedative kept him in a state of light slumber most days, and although she was glad he wasn't in as much pain, Mae wondered how long it would be before he'd come to long enough to speak. To realize what had happened.

They had yet to discuss the amputation. It wasn't clear yet if he even grasped the events of each day.

Once the wound was revealed, she turned and washed her hands thoroughly as doctor Kennedy had instructed and began to cleanse it. It was healing nicely, the flesh knitting together rather smoothly. The physician had done a competent job of removing the bottom portion of John's leg, from the knee down. Mae did not feel any repulsion at seeing the wound. Truth be told the infected gunshot weeks before had been more shocking than this.

A yawn escaped her as she finished cleansing and wrapping the leg. Last thing was to empty the basin. The water sloshed side to side, with each step to the back door. Once she exited the house, she flung the liquid onto the dirt.

When she replaced the basin on the side table, she pulled the sleeping man's blanket up to his chest and smoothed them. She'd wait a few minutes to ensure he did not wake in pain. Collapsing into a chair next to the bed, she watched his chest rise and fall. A few strands of dark hair fell over his well-shaped brows, long lashes fanned over the tops of his cheekbones. Her eyes locked on his slightly parted lips. How soft they'd felt against hers, yet at the same time demanding everything from her, eliciting feelings she'd never experienced.

Another yawn and she decided to close her eyes for a minute.

"Mae?"

John's voice startled her. Sunlight peeked through the curtains. She'd been in the same spot all night, must have fallen asleep. A smile curved her lips at meeting John's clear gray eyes. He studied her with a puzzled expression, and looked about the room.

"Where am I?"

"You and Wesley are here at Hawkins ranch. Don't you remember?" Mae tried to keep her tone light, not wanting to cause him any undue distress. Not yet. The bad news would come soon enough.

"Ranch?" He studied her for a few seconds before continuing. "Yes, I remember now. How long have I been here?"

Oh God. "It's been seven days."

"What?" He started to push to a seated position when she dashed to the bed and pushed him down.

"Don't John! You'll make yourself sick to your stomach. I'll help you up in a few minutes. First take your time and get your bearings."

Alarm filled eyes met hers, before he closed them. "I've been here for a week?"

"Yes."

"What about my son? How is he?"

"He's great, probably in the kitchen charming extra flapjacks out of Elma again."

He brought his arm up over his face and covered his eyes with it. "Mae, I have to speak to you. I have a favor to ask of you. I need you to watch after Wesley for me. I have to get my leg taken care of."

"John," Mae interrupted him moving his arm away from his face. "Look at me."

He did, and this time she could see the old John. An eyebrow cocked, daring her to interrupt him again. "You look tired. You've been caring for your father and me. Probably watching after Wesley too."

"My father died a week ago. And it's not a very flattering observation John McClain." Mae smiled down at him. "Come on let me help you sit up."

"I'm sorry for your loss." John allowed her to help him sit up.

"Don't be, we knew it would happen." She pushed pillows behind his back while he adjusted to sitting, and held her breath knowing any moment now he'd realize the bottom part of his left leg was gone.

"Mae?"

"Yes John."

"It's done?"

"Yes."

He didn't say anything for a long time, and Mae felt at a loss for what she should say to him. Instead she fumbled and pulled at the blankets straightening them to keep her hands busy. Next she went to the basin and filled it with cooled water from the pitcher. After dipping a cloth in to soak it, she wrung it and went back to the bed.

With slow deliberate strokes, she passed the cloth over his face, the entire time his serious eyes remained locked to hers. "I'm not married Mae."

Not sure why he made the statement now, she only nodded.

"Wesley's mother and I met when I was stationed near her home. We began a relationship. I was sent to a remote assignment, so I didn't know she was pregnant, not at first. She contacted my parents, but they didn't tell me anything about it when she refused to meet with them or come to live with them." He took a breath. "They thought she was just looking to get money. In Carla's case it was probably true."

"Where is she now?"

He watched as she ran the cloth down his arms. "Probably headed west to California. She's married now, or so she says. They didn't want to take Wesley along." John cleared his throat, and his brows drew together. "Thank you for caring for him."

Approaching with caution, Mae leaned over him and pressed a kiss to his cheek. "That's what friends do John, we care for one another. Besides, I've fallen in love with Wesley and well... he with me. We were waiting for you to wake up, so we can let you know we're running off together. Into the sunset"

His smile lightened the mood in the room. "He's a lucky man."

Chapter Seventeen

"**H**OW DOES IT feel?" Doctor Kennedy reclined into the chair and waited, his eyes on the leg as John tried to get his balance.

For the first time in many weeks, John stood on two legs and a surge of relief flooded him. It was the first of many steps towards regaining his independence. "It'll take some getting used to." He took a wobbly step with his arms out for balance. "The sooner I can get around, the better so I can help around here."

"Don't get in too much of a hurry," the doctor chuckled. "Mae and Elma both begged me to hold off another week before bringing the prosthetic leg for you. They figured you'd not be patient about getting out and around."

"I appreciate you not listening to them. It's already been almost two months. I'm healed well enough," John replied and took another step. He looked over his shoulder to the open door of the bedroom. "You may as well come in here. I know you're standing there."

Mae peered in, her face flushed. Her eyes flew to his legs. "You're standing on it." She moved with measured slowness toward him with her hands out as if to catch him if he fell.

"Are you in pain?"

"I'm fine." He snapped without looking at her for fear he'd see worry or apprehension. Or worse yet, pity. He'd already made up his mind to work on her ranch through the spring to repay for her taking in him and Wesley. By end of summer he'd find a place of his own where he and his son could live.

"Hmm," Mae's eyebrows drew together and she crossed her arms. "It certainly doesn't improve your disposition much." She turned her attention to the doctor. "Thank you Doctor Kennedy. Any instructions?" As always she was brisk to the task at hand, not letting him get the best of her. He slid a glance at the proud woman who now pointedly ignored him.

The doctor's lips curved and his eyes warmed when he stood to speak to her. The older man was always respectful toward Mae, yet his eyes seemed to drink her in and John didn't begrudge him, after all Mae had such an effect on men. The fact he still felt the urge to growl in frustration when men noticed her beauty annoyed him.

He had no rights to her. It was only a natural reaction. Mae was after all a breathtaking woman.

"Don't overdo it John. If you spend too many hours on the leg one day, you'll pay for it the next. Ease into it. Now take a few more steps and let me see if I need to make any more adjustments. If it's misaligned and you get a sore, it could bring another infection," the doctor instructed.

"I won't Doc. Not in a hurry to see you again, no offense." John took several more assured steps while attempting to disregard Mae's watchful eye.

THE NEXT EVENING, John sat in the kitchen at the table and wondered why suppertime seemed like a festive occasion. Joshua came for dinner and even the usually dour Alan participated in the animated conversation about the upcoming spring festivities in town. Mae and Elma had outdone themselves that night. The table was laden with aromatic food, a roast accompanied by root vegetables flanked by crusty bread and freshly churned butter all smelled and tasted delicious.

When Mae's eyes met his across the table, a ripple of heat traveled down from his chest. He frowned at feeling heat rise to his face. What was wrong with him? How could one look from her affect him so?

Her lips curved knowingly when he grumbled under his breath and adjusted his seat.

"Now for something special," her husky voice did little to settle his already altered state. Mae got up and opened a cupboard to produce a large cake. The dish in hand, she moved with care toward the table, her eyes on him.

Her soft smile made his stomach flip, so he focused on the cake instead. Each day around Mae and able to touch her and share the closeness they once had when on the road. The sooner he and Wesley moved on the better. A man could only resist so long.

Her eyes twinkling, she placed the cake in front of him. "Happy Birthday John."

"What?" He looked around the room and was taken aback. Every set of eyes looked at him with expectation.

"Happy birthday Senor McClain," Elma exclaimed with a broad smile. "Wesley, Senorita Mae and I worked hard on the cake. Hope you like it." She prodded Wesley who tore his eyes from the dessert and looked up at him.

"Hap bird-day Da." The little boy clapped and bounced, his eyes once again glued to the cake.

The changes in Wesley over the last few weeks were astonishing. He'd blossomed into a bright and happy boy. While recovering and unable to leave his room, John heard his son's laughter when the child played in the house. Through the window he often caught sight of the boy running circles around Elma while she worked on the garden or hung clothes on the line. Other times the little boy skipped along hand-in-hand with Mae. Wesley was happy here. How would he react to leaving? John shook the thoughts away and forced a smile. "Thank you. I'd forgotten I told Mae my birthdate when we traveled here."

"Well let's cut it. I can't wait to try it." Mae's face brightened with joy giving him the first glimpse of a different side of her. Jovial and relaxed, she let out a loud laugh when Wesley stood up on his chair and clapped.

The evening progressed, all of them eating too much cake and later each complained about overfilled bellies, but the expressions of cheer contradicted the exaggerated woe filled words. *This is what family should be like.*

Wesley's eyes began to droop and without haste, he was lifted up by Mae and carried to his room. The child laid his head on her shoulder, his tiny arm around her neck. That she'd taken to the boy was more than evident. John wondered if the separation would be harder on her than on his son.

Life sure had a way of throwing one into strange situations,

John pondered. He wouldn't have dreamed of sitting here in a warm kitchen surrounded by people that cared for his child. A child he didn't know up until a few weeks ago. A boy who was now being put to bed by the beautiful woman he fought not to think about every waking moment.

MAE FUMBLED WITH the small package, straightening the blue ribbon yet again. She'd meant to give John the gift earlier when the others had presented him with theirs, but for selfish reasons, she'd abstained. Now she felt rather silly at the thought of wanting to be the only one to witness when John opened it. Although it was but a simple handkerchief she'd embroidered with his initials, each stitch was sewn with meticulous care. It had been so long since they'd spent time alone with only each other for company and she missed him very much. She longed for their quiet conversations and his companionship. So tonight she'd planned to visit with him, sit and talk, just be near to him for a few moments this evening.

The night had been a success. Everyone seemed to have a good time. Even John had smiled more than usual when accepting his gifts. A walking stick from Joshua, a shirt Elma had made him and from Wesley, a pair of socks. She walked into the front room expecting to find John there since he made a habit of sitting by the fireplace in the evenings reading, but the room was empty. Maybe the events of the day had proven too much and he'd decided to retire early?

Although highly inappropriate to go to his bedroom, after traveling together for all those days alone, she no longer gave propriety much thought when it came to John.

"John?" Mae knocked at his bedroom door. Other than a shuffling noise, there was no reply. Her heart quickened. "John, are you all right?"

The door swung open so fast, Mae jumped back stifling a gasp.

His gray eyes were almost black when he looked at her. "What is it Mae?" Well, he certainly seemed none to pleased to see her.

The rejection stung. Of course how foolish she was to think he missed her as much. He had a son to worry about, not to mention just recovering from a shocking loss. Yet tears threatened and she looked away so he would not see. "I'm sorry." Mae took a step back. "Nothing important, I'll speak to you in the morning."

She went to turn, but a firm hand on her elbow stopped her. "Look, it's just that…" he seemed at a loss for words, his eyes searching her face, as if it held the answer. When he noticed the gift in her hand, he eyes widened "Christ, I'm sorry Mae. It's just right now is not a good time for you to be alone with me. I was thinking about you and…I and how we…"

Angrier with herself than him, she tried to pull her arm away. "I apologize for intruding on your evening. Good night John."

Before she could take a step, he swung her around and brought her against his hard chest with such force she feared they'd topple over. Then his lips covered hers with a desperation that took her breath away.

She wrapped her arms around his waist and pulled him

even closer returning his kiss with matched emotions. How she'd missed him, his touch, his warmth during those nights in the back of the wagon.

His mouth moved over hers, and she parted her lips to allow him better access. At once, their tongues automatically twisted around the other.

Mae didn't realize they'd moved into his room until the soft sound of the door closing behind her sounded. The need to be alone with him, to not share any part of who John McClain was, overruled all common sense.

A thought took root in her mind. This was exactly what she needed right now and she made up her mind.

She'd not leave this room tonight.

Then his lips began a lazy trail down to her throat, Mae threw her head back to allow him more access.

"John." The breathless exclamation intermingled with the sounds of their heavy breathing. Her fingers combed into his hair, and she held him in place with one hand while maintaining a hold on his shoulder with the other.

"I want you," John rasped out, his hands slid down her back to cup her derriere and he pushed his thickness into her accentuating the request. "Let me have you Mae."

How could she deny him? She'd already made the decision and the reply was easy.

"Yes." Mae's answer came like a deep moan followed by a sharp intake of breath when he managed to expose her breasts and began to lap at one while his fingers play with the other. Sensations slammed into her, and she could just barely keep upright. Yet she pulled her fingers through his hair in encouragement, desperate for him not to stop.

John growled and pushed her back onto his bed, falling with her to land on top of her.

His weight brought back memories of their time together on the trail. He smelled of outdoors and rain, his scent igniting her further and she pulled at his shirt needing to touch his skin. Finally when the garment came loose from his pants, she ran her fingers under it running her palms across his broad back and then across the expanse of his chest. All the while, his darkened eyes bore into hers as he allowed her free access to his body.

HE'D SUPPRESSED THE desire for Mae far too long, and now with her in his bed, John was not going to allow the enticing woman out of it until he claimed her. To hell with the repercussions he'd have to face tomorrow.

The fiery trail her fingers left across his skin only added fuel to the already tenuous hold on his urges, and John pressed himself against her center to find her reciprocating with an upward thrust of her hips.

Fearing he was too heavy, he rolled onto his back so that she lay over him. She peered down at him, her long blonde hair a tangled mess, and he took pride in being responsible for her disheveled appearance. He took her swollen lips once again and ran his fingers through the silky tresses, loosening them to fall down past her shoulders.

The reverberations of their breathing and the sound of their kissing merged with the rustling of clothing. Mae's skirts and blouse joined his shirt on the floor.

John hesitated to remove his pants, but the decision was taken away when her delft fingers began making short work of the fastenings at his waist. She pushed the garment down past his hips, her gaze trailing behind studying the exposed skin. When moving to where his left leg ended. His heart beat faster and he stayed her hand. Frozen he couldn't move forward, John even stopped breathing, the last breath stuck in his throat.

"I can't"

Breathing began again with gulps, and he moved backward, his hands still holding his pants up and covering the evidence of his arousal. John kept his gaze down to the floor focusing on the strewn clothes.

"I find you totally and completely perfect John," her husky words had the wrong effect. Of course she was just trying to make him feel better, acted as if the fact he was not whole did not matter to sooth his ego. It was all an act for his sake, and he was not convinced. Perhaps she did want him at the moment, and he attempted to take a step forward, but could not. Finally he was able to swallow past the constriction in his throat and he looked at her.

Her face although still flushed now held nothing but tenderness and it made him feel even less worthy of her. "Come here John. Nothing has to happen between us if you are not ready, but please come back to me." She'd pulled the blanket over herself, and he hated he could no longer see her perfect body.

John released a slow exhalation as he neared the bed and lay back onto it.

On her side, she rested her head on her hand, her gaze flickering to him and then around the room. "This is my first time in this bed."

His gaze traveled to her parted lips. "I've wanted you since that day. The day I walked you home."

"The day you hurried off without looking back?" Her lips curved upward and she slid her fingers over his shoulder. "I remember the day."

"I want to kiss you again Mae."

Her eyes locked onto his, and she leaned forward. "Then kiss me John."

THEIR LIPS JOINED again with him, not allowing any thought to linger on the fact he was not a whole man. With her right now in his bed, a luckier more complete man did not exist. He pulled her over him ensuring the blankets remained in place and held her close.

John leaned his forehead against hers, the whispers of her breathing fanning across his face. "I'm sorry."

"Don't apologize John. I shouldn't have come here, rushed you." She moved to lie beside him and placed her head on his shoulder.

"You attempted to take advantage of me." John's highbrow expression of shock made her grin.

"Truly, I didn't expect more than you to open my gift."

"A better gift you could not have given me than to spend time, be here with me right now. I missed being alone with you."

Her smile brightened the room, her happy expression making his chest swell. It almost made up for the fact that he was not able to be with her as a man.

JOHN'S BROW CREASED and she could tell he thought about what happened, so she stroked his face and turned him to her. "This is what I really wanted too. I too missed those long days on the road with you when we spent hours together."

His somber eyes bore into hers. "Have you ever... God, how do I phrase this? Have you ever been with someone like me? Not whole?"

The words weighed on her, but she could not blame him for not knowing the truth of her life since she lived in a brothel. After all, it was common knowledge most madams started off a working girls.

"No I have not," she replied truthfully. "I've had a lover, and he had two legs, both worked perfectly."

"A lover?"

"Yes John, I never sold my body for a price. If I took a lover once, it was because I'll never marry and wanted to know what it was like between men and women. Even if only temporary."

A long silence followed, with neither speaking for a long time. Finally, John placed a kiss onto her forehead and let out a sigh. "What happened between you?"

"He ended it of course. It goes without saying, that although I was a virgin our first night, he still found me unworthy of marriage."

John frowned, his eyes locked to hers. "I have to know how this is possible. You own a brothel, you're a…"

"Madam," Mae replied and attempted to slide away, but his arm remained firm holding her in place. "Both my mother and Miss Lady demanded I keep from serving customers. In their minds, they thought one day a proper gentleman would show interest in me and ask for my hand in marriage." The bitterness in her voice surprised her, yet she plundered on. "As you well understand, it will never happen. Not for me. Virgin or not, I'm a tarnished woman."

He held her tight. "I can't marry you either Mae. But it's not what…."

Her heart lurched at the words, and body stiffened. "I wouldn't ask you to."

"Yet it would be the proper thing to do," John replied letting out a breath.

"I would never ask it of you or expect it. I'm sure for someone like you to marry someone of my social standing is unthinkable." She moved away from him and this time he allowed it.

John remained quiet, deep in thought for a moment. "It's not what you think Mae, I have to figure out how to deal with all this," he motioned to his leg. "And I have a son to worry about now. I don't have anything to offer you."

Mae rolled to her side facing him. "Can this night not be about expectations? Let's just talk."

"I can give us that," he replied.

Then he kissed her, the soft kiss was meant to reassure her, but instead it shattered her heart and soul.

Chapter Eighteen

IT WAS UNUSUALLY hot for April, at least John thought so, he wasn't sure it was his first time there. Waves of heat pulsated from the parched ground but fortunately the clouds gathering in the otherwise bright blue sky promised a reprieve. Plus the rains would ensure a healthy crop.

John pushed his hat up from his brow, wiping absently with his handkerchief and listened to Alan, who explained the need for another field horse.

He'd fallen naturally into the role of overseer. Once training John to his satisfaction, Joshua was free to work his own lands and had gladly relinquished the duties over to him.

While listening, John glanced over at the other two men they'd hired recently. The men took a break under a shade tree, both drinking heavily of the cool water Elma had brought out. "I certainly understand why you feel another horse is necessary, but the three we have seem more than sufficient. However, I will speak to the Joshua to see if he also feels one of the horses is as unsuitable as you suspect." He replied. "Tell the others we have to get the equipment gathered and into the barn before the rains come." He dismissed the man and headed toward the stable. Alan, a hard worker, he seemed satisfied with John's reply and went to join the others.

John looked past the fields toward the horse corrals where several colts pranced around the adults.

Virginia was no longer an option, his father had written, he was selling the press. Perhaps he'd remain here, he'd start a new life for Wesley and himself.

A small farm, with stables.

Once settled, he'd see about breeding horses. Raising his purebreds was where his true passion lay. The experience here at Hawkins' ranch was a boon. He'd learned quite a bit about not only the proper way to run a large estate, but about horse breeding as well. At five years his senior, Joshua took him through the paces of all involved in running the ranch and all he knew about horses. It was evident the soft-spoken man had learned from the best.

John admired what Mae's father had acquired here and the hard work that must have gone into prospering such a great ranch.

The rain began to fall in earnest just an hour later, and John made his way from the stables to the house. His leg bothered him enough to let him know he'd spent too much time moving about that day. This evening he planned on a hot bath and perhaps reading in the front room. *How easily I've become domesticated.* He smiled at the thought and shook his head. Just months earlier, he much preferred spending the evening outdoors to being inside.

This could be his life, a future with Mae. But no, not only would he not burden Mae with his deformity and a child to boot, but also the thought of encroaching on her land as well sickened him.

Although Mae and he had remained civil toward each other since the night she'd spent in his bed, a curtain had fallen between them. He wasn't certain if he or she had done the honors of hanging it, but there it remained. Soft, yet still a barrier separating them nonetheless.

She deserved a whole man, and he would not stand in the way of her finding someone who would love her unconditionally. Regardless of how she'd made him feel on the night she'd come to his bedroom, as if his deformity did not matter, it did.

It had to.

Then there was the obstacle of her tarnished background. No matter how much he tried, it was impossible for him to ignore it. That someone would look upon her as before, a prostitute if she ever were to become his wife was something he could not reconcile. What would his reaction be? Was it fair for others to judge her? For him to?

She'd only had one other lover. How was it possible? She had no reason to lie. And he believed her, but for some reason it did not change the picture of her in his mind.

A scene repeated in his mind of the interior of the brothel. Tinny piano music playing, while the smoke and chatter of people filled the already overcrowded room. Presiding over the space like a royal, Mae stood out in spite of the colorful clothing of the other woman. With Kohl-lined eyes and feather in her hair, she reined over the establishment, a beautiful seductive madam.

And what about him? The desire of his heart was to have a wife, a family and a life something just like the current one here with Mae and Wesley at Hawkins ranch. His leg pulsed in reply.

Although Mae hadn't recoiled at the sight of his missing limb when she'd taken care of him, he'd felt its absence. No longer able to walk without a limp, he hated the lack of smoothness in his stride.

No. A life here was not for him. Most women expected more from their husband.

Not for you.

Having rounded the house and walked to the front, John neared the porch and peered through the window. He looked through the large picture window and stopped in his steps, taking a minute to soak in the scene before him.

He could not tear his eyes away from the interior. Mae sat in an overstuffed chair before the fireplace with Wesley in her lap holding a book, their heads so close together they touched. The little boy traced lines along the page as she read out loud to him. Before long, his hands fell away and Wesley burrowed into the woman who the little boy had come to see as a mother figure. He thrust his thumb in his mouth while Mae continued with the story.

John remained transfixed, remorse shoring into his chest at the knowledge he'd separate the two very soon. The guilt grew upon spotting Wesley wrapping his little fingers around Mae's wrist seeking the security of her to hold him after he fell asleep.

As if sensing his watch, Mae turned to the window then quickly away. But not before he caught sight of a tear trailing down her cheek.

It was best he find a way to leave without delay.

"So soon?" Mae twisted her hands in her apron. The flour from the bread she was making leaving a dusty print.

Elma nodded, her lips pressed together. "Yes, Senor McClain told me this morning before he left to go into town. He is going to look at a property to buy. And that he hoped to move in a couple of weeks."

"Well I suppose it's to be expected," Mae trailed off when Wesley rushed into the room and threw his arms around her legs.

"Go walk!" He announced looking up at her with anticipation. It had become their routine after she'd finished her morning chores to go outside and walk while teaching him words and spelling. "Not now Wes, in a few minutes." She leaned down and placed a kiss on top of his head.

He looked to Elma and she held out a cookie for him. "Go wait on the porch and eat it," she instructed him watching with fondness as he scampered out the door.

Mae blinked away the moisture in her eyes. She'd come to think of this as a permanent life. She'd written Miss Lady to inform her she'd decided to remain in Texas indefinitely, inviting her to come out to visit. It would do Miss Lady good to get away from the brothel and spend time here.

Now she wondered at her plans. What would her life be after John and Wesley left? Would she wish to remain in Texas? She caught sight of Wesley on the back porch nibbling at his cookie and she wondered if John would allow the boy to remain with her. After all, he could not possible complete all the duties involved in starting a horse farm and hiring men while caring for his young son at the same time.

The idea of approaching him to allow Wesley to remain there for an indefinite period made her feel much better and she finished by placing the dough into a bowl to rise then wiped her hands.

"I'm going for a walk with the handsome gentleman who stares at us through the window," she announced.

Elma looked to see Wesley's face pressed against the glass and burst out laughing. "He is not a very patient man, now is he?"

"So much like his father," Mae replied shaking her head.

Elma stopped her with a light touch to her upper arm. "Senorita, you can stop Senor McClain from leaving. Why do you not accept him as your husband?"

"He's never asked Elma. I believe he is not interested in marriage." Mae gave Elma an even look. "Even if he was, he knows my past Elma." Mae swallowed hard past the lump forming in her throat. "And cannot forget it, I'm afraid. John would never marry me."

"I don't know what your past is," Elma huffed. "But I know love when I see it, and that man loves you."

"Not enough apparently." Mae untied her apron and went to leave. Stalling at Elma's next words.

"We will see."

Just as Mae went outside Alan, approached, the man hurried to where she stood holding Wesley by the hand. It was hard to read the large man, his quiet reserve a shield. He frowned at her and took a breath as if not sure what to say.

"What is it Alan?"

The man looked to the child. "Someone is here," his eyes remained on Wesley. "You should see about it alone Miss Mae."

Without asking anything further, she guided Wesley back inside instructing Elma who'd come to see what happened to keep him inside and out of sight.

Alan removed his hat and scratched his head. "Miss Mae, there's a woman out front. Came in a wagon. She's claimin' to be the boy's mama. Said she wants to talk to Mr. John. I told her he was gone, but she insists on talkin' to someone."

Wesley's mother?

Mae straightened her shoulders and brushed the flour from her skirts, then ran an expert hand over her hair to ensure all was in place. "Thank you Alan. Please come with me, and remain a short distance away while I speak to her."

Thankful for the man's size, Mae walked alongside Alan his presence reassuring. They went through the house and exited the front door onto the porch. Alan stood a few feet away to safeguard her if the woman decided to over-react.

Her years of working in the brothel brought with it an innate knowledge of people, the cause for actions and words. And no time was Mae more thankful for it than upon meeting Carla.

Mae kept the knowledge of knowing the woman's name to herself. Instead stood just outside the door and motioned for the woman to join her on two chairs on the front porch. "How can I help you?"

Although attractive, the woman was very thin and harsh in

appearance and with her speech. Her serviceable clothing although well tended to and clean, were old. Mae noted fraying at the hems of the brown skirt. The telltale sign of a hard life was evident in the manner of her posture and lack of luster in her skin and hair. Her shrewd eyes took a fast inventory of both Mae's face and clothing before agreeing to sit. "I'm Carla, Wesley's mother," she stated without giving indication of the purpose for her visit.

It struck Mae as odd how the woman had not asked to see Wesley right away. Instead of saying anything, Mae remained silent, not introducing herself.

"I've come to get Wesley." "I'm moving west and have decided it's best to take the boy with me."

The boy. Not "my son" or "my child".

"I'm afraid the decision is up to John McClain, and as you've been told, he is away, gone to town for the day. You can return tomorrow and speak to him." Mae remained still, giving the impression of calmness with her hands folded on her lap. Her steady hands gave no indication of the pounding in her chest. She looked over to see the woman had driven up in a serviceable wagon and came alone.

"I don't have time to wait another day," Carla told her leaning forward. "We're starting a new life. My husband and I. He's ready to leave, but the more I think about it, I want him along. I refused to go without Wesley."

Mae cleared her throat and slid her gaze to ensure Alan remained a few short yards away. "I'm afraid I will not budge on this matter, like I told you, return tomorrow."

"The fact you're shacked up with John McClain does not

give you any say over this. I came to take the boy and will not leave until you hand him over." Carla sneered and jumped to her feet. "I don't have time to waste coming back here." She shrieked, but took a step back when Alan cleared his throat.

When the woman looked inside the house, her eyes narrowing in calculation. It was then Mae understood the true purpose of her visit. "You people with all your money have no idea what it's like to travel so far and not have enough to make it. That's why we are going west. There ain't no money to be made here."

"How much would it take to get you to leave without Wesley and never return?"

Carla was shrewd enough to lower eyes to hide any gleam of greed, but when she licked at her upper lip it became obvious.

Mae fought to understand how easily the woman would give up the beautiful little boy. "How much?"

"Well I do care deeply for my child."

Mae almost laughed out loud.

The woman had yet to ask to see Wesley.

"Alan, please keep the lady company. I will return shortly." Mae stood and went inside to fetch the payment. Anger simmered in her gut, but she kept it at bay. No use in showing the woman how much the visit affected her. When John returned, she'd beg him that Wesley would never learn of this. The pitiful amount the woman demanded almost made her want to pay more just to prove how much Wesley was worth.

Chapter Nineteen

JOHN WATCHED ON as Elma and Mae made a big production out of putting Wesley to bed. The boy was definitely doted upon and would be a handful for him once they moved. Yet he didn't interfere knowing this was one battle he'd not win.

Once tucked in, the tired but still smiling boy looked over to him and held his arms out. "Night Da."

As was customary, he went to the bed and leaned over to hug his son. "Good night Son." Wesley held on to his neck and sighed. John wondered at the boys' thoughts at times. Whenever John was within his sights, Wesley tracked his movements, always watching where he went. He'd hoped by now to have proven to the child he'd not leave him, but sometimes he wondered if there was another reason why Wesley watched him so closely. Perhaps he'd ask Elma her opinion. The woman had told him she'd raised four sons.

"I must speak to you," Mae caught up to him in the hall-way. "It's important." She went past him towards the front room and he followed.

Her perfume assailed his senses when he entered the room. Mae closed the door behind them, and John steeled himself against the urge to reach for her, to touch her. Even in her sensible pale green calico dress, her stand was regal and she was breathtaking as always.

What a fool he'd been to think he'd be better able to keep a distance from Mae. He'd actually believed once he'd kissed her again and the illusion was broken, he'd be able to remain impassive.

Quite the opposite, he'd craved her with a hunger that constantly gnawed at him.

The beauty moved across the room, and she stood by the window, her hand on the drapes. While Mae processed whatever she would speak to him about, John took full advantage and studied her profile at leisure. Had he'd noticed how her slightly upturned nose fit her face so perfectly before? She pressed her full lips together for a moment and then faced him. "A woman claiming to be Wesley's mother was here today."

His stomach sank. "Why wasn't I alerted about this as soon as I returned?" He stalked to where she stood and scowled down at her. "What happened? Did she see Wesley?"

Mae took a step backward and stepped on the hem of her skirts. She wobbled and threw her hands out to get her balance. John held her steady until she regained her stability. When she straightened, their faces only a scant inch apart both froze, gazes locked.

Seconds ticked by while they faced off, neither wanting to be the first to move away. *Stubborn woman.*

John looked away first and motioned to the couch. "The ride to and from town took its toll. I have to sit down."

"Of course, goodness, I didn't think on it. Let's sit."

He cringed at the instant concern in her tone and followed her to the chairs flanking the fireplace sitting across from her. "Now tell me what happened please."

Mae took a breath. "I had Alan stand by while I met with her out front and instructed Elma to keep Wesley out of sight. The woman, Carla, contended her reason for coming was to take Wesley with her out west. I informed her I could not allow it. That it was your decision to make. After several more exchanges, where she claimed not to be able to return another day to speak to you, I offered her payment in exchange for leaving permanently. Without Wesley."

John searched her face. "Why would you do that?"

Mae shrugged. "The woman never once asked to see her son. I am a good judge of character. By the way she sized up my clothing and the house, I knew she was more interested in money than in seeing him."

"Did she take it then?"

"Of course," Mae shook her head. "Honestly John, I don't see any of her in Wesley. I don't know what your relationship is with her, but I must apprise you she insinuated to be married to the outlaw."

"She must be then," John answered then met her questioning look.

"Do you think she'll return again? I mean how can she just leave her son?"

"I didn't get the opportunity to know Carla enough to claim to understand her motivations or what she'll do. From what I understood from her sister, she's always been a bit of a free spirit. After she contacted my parents when Wesley was born, they exchanged correspondence with a solicitor. My parents did not care for her reputation for taking lovers. I wanted to find the child and see for myself whether or not he was mine since it seemed questionable I was the father."

"Yet you went to great lengths to find him," Mae stated. "It's a good thing you did, because there is no question. Wesley is your son."

"Yes he is." He couldn't stop the smile at speaking of his son. "Tell me the amount you paid her, I will repay you of course."

She told him the amount, and it was a much smaller amount than he expected. Pleading eyes met his. "John, promise me you'll never tell Wesley about this." Her concern for his son touched him and he was forced to clear his throat. Mae was such a caring soul.

"Of course, don't worry Mae. He will never learn about it. If I can help it, he will never meet her either."

"Thank you," she placed her hand over his, the warmth of it ran up his arm to settle in his chest. "Tell me about your day."

John nodded and looked into Mae's eyes only to find a mixture of curiosity and sadness. "My trip to town was to see about a property I learned was for sale. I found it to be a small piece of land with a small serviceable house. I plan to purchase it once my money is transferred to the bank in town. I will also repay you then as well."

"Elma told me this morning of your plans. I would like to propose that until you are settled, Wesley remain here." Without giving him time to reply, she launched into the next statement. "He has been through enough John. Once you get your house into acceptable shape, you will be required to work long hours to get everything prepared for the winter. Then there is the matter of hiring a caregiver. You must find someone who is trustworthy to care for Wesley and see about his studies."

She loved his son. John settled back in his chair, enjoying the fire in her eyes as she made the case she'd no doubt practiced. Her chest heaved with every breath as her passionate pleas fell away from her lips. "John, please think on it, I am not asking for an answer this instant. I do understand it would be hard for you to be away from Wesley, but we can arrange to come and spend time with you or you can come and sup regularly. I don't want to take him from you…I just want…"

"I understand," John interrupted her. "And I'm grateful you care for my boy as much as you do. But you have to understand, the longer he remains here, the harder it will be for him to come away with me." He hesitated when tears sprang to her eyes. "Mae, it's going to be a painful transition for everyone involved. I am not so uncaring not to know how you feel. I will think on this and make a decision. But I have to decide based on what I feel will be best for Wesley." He covered her hand with his and once again was forced to hold back the need to move it further up her soft skin. "Thank you for loving my boy so much."

Mae slipped her hand from under his and stood. "Very well. Good night John."

"Senorita, there is a wagon approaching." Elma came into the front room where Mae sat mending the next day. She dropped her sewing into the basket at her feet and went to the window.

Indeed a wagon approached, a couple sat on the bench, the man guiding the horses toward the house.

"It's the Jacobs'!" With a shriek of laughter, Mae ran to the front door and out to meet the wagon.

No sooner did the wagon stop than Patty dressed in a red calico dress and matching bonnet, practically flew off of it and went to embrace Mae who was already standing to the side. The women hugged, stood back and looked at each other with broad smiles only to hug again. Ryan remained back and held the horse's reins, smiling at their antics while patiently waiting for Mae to turn her attention to him.

"Oh Ryan, thank you for bringing my friend to see me," Mae finally rushed to him and they also embraced.

Arms entwined around each other's waists, the women made their way to the house, while one of the ranch hands came to show Ryan where the stables were.

"Of course you plan to stay for a few days?" Mae asked barely able to get her breath, "I missed you so."

Patty wiped at tears of happiness. "If it's not an imposition, we brought provisions so we could stay in the wagon if necessary."

"I won't hear of it." Mae tugged her friend toward the kitchen where Elma was already preparing a light fare for the guests. "Oh Patty, I have so much to tell you, and want to know everything. I can't wait to hear about your new home."

Patty sat and accepted a glass of lemonade proffered by Elma and smiled up at her.

"Oh excuse my manners," Mae exclaimed. "Patricia Jacobs this is Elma. She was my father's caregiver. And she's remained here as a godsend to me."

Elma's puffed her chest with pride at her words. "Senorita Mae is a saint."

Alan came to announce Ryan remained in the stables visiting with John, so Patty ate a small repast while Mae kept her company bringing her up to date on what had transpired since they'd parted ways.

Patty then informed her they'd established into a small home less than a day's ride away. Ryan's father was having a hard time relinquishing the church over to his son. Instead of participating in the tug-of-war with him, she and Ryan were planting a new church near their home. Mae clapped at the news. They'd be closer, and she could see her friend regularly.

After Patty ate the small meal, they moved to the front room and continued their discussion. Patty's keen eyes took Mae in. "I notice a certain sadness in your eyes, in spite of your initial joy at seeing me. What happened between you and John?"

"It's what I've come to expect," Mae replied. "He's moving, taking his darling son with him. He's come to care for me Patty, I am sure of it. Although, I am not sure he loves me enough to marry me even without the obstacle of my past."

"I'm so sorry," Patty shook her head. "Men can be so pig-headed. I mean why does he not see his son needs a mother and accept he loves you. And unless things have changed, John

McClain does." Patty huffed. "And to think he plans to rip that child away from you. It makes me so angry."

Mae smiled at seeing the diminutive women hit her fist into the palm of the other hand. "Please Patty, let's leave the conversation for another day. Tell me, are you with child yet?"

Patty's eyes glistened with unshed tears. "I am beginning to think God is never going to bless us with a child."

JOHN STOOD BY and watched the stable hand shoe the new workhorse. His stomach rumbled, and he wondered at the time.

"Well there you are," Ryan Jacobs approached, a soft curve to his lips. "It's good to see you John."

Genuinely glad to see the familiar face, John went to greet the man and they shook hands. "Well, it's great to see you. I wondered how long it would be before you and Patricia would come and see about Mae. She's mentioned once or twice at wanting to come to see you."

"To be honest, if it were up to my wife, we'd come a month ago. She's been anxious to see her friend. Driving me crazy with it actually." The warmth in Ryan's eyes told he was happy to indulge his wife.

"You are still limping," Ryan stated. "Is the leg still giving you problems?"

"Not as much," John replied and knocked on the wooden lower part. "Not as much friend."

Ryan laughed.

Once the men made their way back, they walked into to a house full of activity. Mae helped Patricia settle their things into her father's old bedroom while Wesley immediately took to Ryan, the boy showing him his collection of wooden horses.

The conversation over dinner flowed easily, and John was surprised to find how much he missed the Jacob's company. They were an amazing couple whose easy-going personalities brought ease.

Mae eyes were brighter, and she smiled more than she'd done in days. The visit was a great distraction for them after the countless days of tension.

This could be his life. He was fully aware of it, yet he could not take deny what he'd knew. Upon studying Mae when she stood to get the pot of coffee, full of elegance and grace, he felt stronger about his decision. She deserved a whole man, a better man than he could ever be.

TWO DAYS LATER, they ate outside, an impromptu picnic planned by the women.

Although the air was brisk, it remained warm enough outdoors so the party lingered outdoors after the meal. The ladies had brought out a Sears and Roebuck catalog, their heads together as they studied the pictures, while Wesley, who'd worn himself out playing, napped on a blanket nearby.

Ryan joined John a short distance away where he fished, more to pass the time than to catch anything, it was too late in the day for it. "These are beautiful lands."

"That they are," John agreed. "A perfect place to live."

"John?" Ryan got his attention. "I know you're not married to Mae. I also know why you said you were and I understand why you did."

John continued to fish wondering what Ryan planned to say next.

"Patty tells me you plan to purchase land nearby and move with Wesley?" Ryan pushed his hands into his pocket and brought out a jackknife. He bent to pick up a stick, giving John time to reply.

"It was my plan all along, to find my son, maybe start a family and settle down. I didn't plan to lose a leg and become a cripple in the process." His line became tangled and John wiggled the pole and tugged it. "So, yes it's true, just earlier this week, I found a place, plan to make an offer on it."

"I see," Ryan replied, his knife making short work of the small stick he held. "What about your life here? It seems to me, you have the perfect family already?"

John followed Ryan's line of sight to where the women sat. "Mae deserves a whole man for a husband."

"Is that what she says?"

John remained silent, not ready to share his reservations about her background and of the backlash a marriage to someone with a stigma like hers attached.

"You know," Ryan began. "The Lord says there is no one sin bigger than another. A sin just is. Whether you commit a sin or judge a sinner who does, both are the same."

"I admit I am nowhere near perfect, but I do try," John replied. "But some things are hard to move beyond."

"Yes, it's hard for us as humans to change the way we think and feel about what others may think, say or do. Especially when it comes to certain professions." Ryan lifted his eyes to meet his, and John felt his own widen. *He knew.*

"But," Ryan continued, his attention back to the whittling. "An honorable person will look into another's character and see them for who they are. Certainly love helps." Ryan threw what was left of the stick down. "Seems to me the problem is here." He pressed his fingers to the center of John's chest.

"I need to drag my wife back and get packing so we can make our leave at dawn. Hopefully we can get home before too late. I have much to do."

John pulled the line from the water and held out his hand. "I look forward to coming to your church. You are a rare man Ryan Jacobs. Someone I have come to think of as a friend."

With a smile Ryan shook his head. "Well I try. Just think on what I've said. Maebelle is one of the most generous, kindhearted women my wife and I have ever met. It'd be a shame for prejudice stand in the way of a relationship with her."

"Like I said, she deserves a whole man, not a cripple," John forced himself to keep his gaze from wandering away from the man's who stood before him.

"And like I said, you should let her decide," Ryan curved into his signature soft smile, and he hugged John's shoulder before both headed back to where the women were now packing the picnic items.

John watched as Mae laughed at something Patricia said, then turned and gathered Wesley into her arms.

He had to leave, perhaps sooner than later, else he'd find it impossible to do so.

Chapter Twenty

MAE STIRRED CREAM into her tea and listened to John and Elma discussing his questions regarding Wesley's propensity to always watch him so closely.

Elma answered while moving about completing her chores. "Senor, I think it's more he admires you. Most little boys want to grow up to be like their father, so they study closely while growing up. My boys did the same with their father."

John's eyes slid to her, but she decided it was best to abstain from commenting, as she'd never spent much time around children other than Wesley. How she'd taken naturally to John's son surprised her.

"I'm relieved to hear it Elma, thank you. Well ladies, I have to go see about the harvest. It's almost done. Once everything is gone to market, there will be more time for rest." He cleared his throat. "Mae, have you decided who you will hire as overseer? Alan is a good candidate. Not much needed to be done in order to train him to take my place."

With practiced perfection, Mae kept from showing any emotion. "Yes, I have to find a good substitute for you, John." She emphasized the word *you* and he arched a brow obviously understanding her underlying meaning. "I will hire Alan as the overseer."

"He will be glad to hear it," John's clipped reply made her gloat inside at the small victory of a direct hit.

"I'll let him know about it later today," Mae told him a smile curving her lips. She would not let him know how much his impending departure hurt. She leaned forward and peered at him. "Does this mean you've come up with a departure date? What about Wesley?"

"Yes," John blinked and looked around. Elma had walked out, giving them privacy. "When we go into town tomorrow, I will inquire as to my funds and the land. I don't foresee it being much longer than a week at most."

"It gives you plenty of time to go over things with Alan and since the other two men will be done for the most part with their chores. Feel free to hire them to help you set up. I think Alan can cover things here. If need be, I'll help him with any matters which come up."

"You?" John growled out. "What do you know about ranching?"

"I can learn," she stuck her chin out at him. "What about Wesley?" She repeated keeping her voice level.

"I agree with you. It's best he remain here for the time being. I'd like to make arrangements between us so I can see him regularly. I am grateful you offered to care for him." John stood.

Mae followed suite. "He can stay as long as necessary. As a matter of fact, I'm hopeful that you will allow me to continue to see him. I know that once he is older you may have some reservations, yet I care for him."

"Of course," John replied. His abrupt words did not tell his thoughts.

Satisfied that at least she'd keep Wesley, Mae relaxed. "Speaking of which, I best go see if he's awake. Have a good day John."

John's hand on her elbow stopped her and Mae looked down at him.

His gaze searched her face. "I don't know what to say to you Mae. This is not an easy thing for me."

"What are you trying to tell me John that you haven't already made plain? You may care for me, but whatever obstacles you've created are too large to get over."

He looked away, but remained silent.

Furious now, she shrugged her arm out of his hand and left the kitchen.

THE HORSES' CANTER along with the light breeze made the trip to town the next day enjoyable. For the most part lost in his thoughts, John tried to keep from looking to his right side where Mae sat. They went to town together, John guiding the horses while Mae sat next to him on the bench with enough space between them to fit a basket. He knew this because she'd placed one there upon sitting down.

The ride, though just a couple hours, brought back memories of their time together all those days to get to Texas, and John was pressed not to recall the many things which happened since. He slid a glance at Mae. She sat relaxed with a serene expression on her face.

"Miss Lady's visit not too long after the Jacobs' must make you happy. It will fill the emptiness after the Jacobs' departure," John told her in hopes of starting a conversation no involving his eminent departure.

Mae's smile showcased her deep dimples. "Yes it does. I have missed her so much. She brings Lucinda, her daughter with her since she felt uncomfortable traveling for such a long distance alone."

"How long will she remain?"

"I don't know. I hope indefinitely. There is much to decide and talk about. Once she gets settled, I will ask her to remain at least as long as I do."

She still planned to leave. "I didn't know you were planning to return east." John kept his tone remained neutral in spite of the now rapid heartbeat.

"I don't know yet for sure. Part of me has grown to like Hawkins' lands, but when you and Wesley move and Miss Lady leaves, I may grow lonely. I am not sure I want to remain here with only Elma for company. Like I said there is much to decide." Mae leaned forward when the town came into view. "Oh dear it looks like the stagecoach has arrived. I hope they've not waited too long." She rubbed her palms on her skirts and shifted in her seat.

John smiled at her excitement. "It looks to me they've only just arrived. Look they are still unloading the baggage." He found a place and reigned in the horses, then climbed down and helped Mae to do so as well. He held her hand as she ascended, the warmth of it taking him by surprise. Mae hesitated before drawing it away, but accepted his arm to lead her across the packed dirt walkway to the stagecoach station.

Several townspeople turned and greeted them, most of them casting curious glances at them and then whispering to each other about who they were. No doubt, they'd heard of Hawkins' daughter, but from the looks of regard, talks of her beauty had not done her justice. Oblivious to the stares, Mae greeted several folks with warm smiles and even stopped to admire a woman's baby, much to the young mother's delight.

Miss Lady waited outside the station. She stood with her back straight and waited for them to approach. With a squeal of delight, Mae threw her arms around the diminutive lady and kissed her face. "Oh Miss Lady, I have missed you so much," Mae wiped an errant tear away. "I can't believe you're here." She turned a bright smile on John and he went to greet Miss Lady.

"Well look at you Captain McClain. You look well recovered," Miss Lady regarded him up and down. "I'd say living out west suits you well."

John kissed her cheek and picked up her bag. "Thank you Miss Lady, how was your travel?"

"Too long for this old woman, just too long," Miss Lady replied taking Mae's arm and walking briskly toward the wagon, not seeming to be tired at all. Lucinda, who John remembered from the brothel, picked up the other bag and followed behind them, her bright red dress and saunter causing several townsmen to take notice.

The ride back was filled with chatter, the women catching up what occurred since they'd left Virginia. John remained quiet, only answering when they asked him something directly. Mae told Miss Lady about her father's dying and described the ranch and each of the people who worked there. When she described Joshua, John couldn't help but noticed she went into significantly more detail, telling of his height, hair, color and body build.

Miss Lady asked him about Wesley, when Mae told her about his son, but as usual the woman was wise enough not to ask the nature of his relationship with his son's mother. Although Mae did not tell Miss Lady of what happened to his leg, John got the impression her discerning eyes had already figured it out.

Upon approaching the ranch, the two newcomers gushed about the beauty of the lands and house, which made John study the sight before him as well. The pecan tree lined road to the ranch house was indeed picturesque and the soft rolling hills, upon where horses and cattle grazed definitely gave a sense of wellbeing. This was what he envisioned his home would evolve to once he purchased it and worked it a few years. Not as large, but he intended to make it prosper.

Chapter Twenty-One

A LAN WAITED WITH Elma behind the house when John pulled the cart with the visitors around to the back. Once they stopped, he went to the rear to unload the trunks only to stop when a slender woman joined him and began tugging at a smaller one.

"I've got this ma'am," he told her while at the same time putting his hand out the stop the trunk from sliding.

Almond shaped eyes met his, and the woman huffed taking a step back. "Fine, if you want to break your back then go ahead."

At a loss for words, he could only stare at her. In a bright red dress, with short matching gloves, the slight woman looked to weigh much less than the trunk she'd attempted to unload. Flawless caramel skin, her heart shaped face was framed by dark curls. She brought a gloved hand over her brow to shade her eyes from the sun and raised an eyebrow at him. "Why are you looking at me like that?"

"I—I'm sorry miss, you took me by surprise." He felt his face heat up and turned away to the trunks. "I'll get this right in if you wish to go on in."

She didn't move, actually seemed reluctant to follow Mae,

Elma and the older woman who were already in the kitchen. Arms filled with parcels, John followed after them and went inside.

"My name is Lucinda Roberts," she said.

The truck was heavy, but he held it without moving toward the house. "It's a pleasure to meet you. I'm Alan Murphy."

Lucinda didn't smile. "Yes, well I suppose I should go on in." Her eyes lingered toward the house, but she did not move.

Alan placed the trunk back on the wagon. "Why don't we walk a bit? I can show you around."

Relief poured from her and she bobbed her head up and down. "I would like that. It's a nice day, thank you."

When she slipped her hand through his arm, a sensation like of finally taking a deep breath after holding it for years, took him by surprise. He guided her away from the house toward the paddock so she could see the horses and colts grazing. They stopped before a fence and she placed her hands on it seeming to take it all in. "It's beautiful here." She blinked several times and took a shaky breath. "Momma needs to be here."

"What about you?"

There was a challenge in her eyes when she straightened her shoulders and met his stare dead on. Gone was any sign of vulnerability, any softness. Like clouds taking away sunshine, shadows covered any sign of openness. "I don't belong anywhere." The curve to her lips being more cruel than friendly caught his attention. "Except maybe the brothel from which I just came from."

When he didn't react, her mouth opened slightly, both

eyebrows rose. She was beautiful. Alan allowed his mouth to curve into a rare smile. "Sometimes fate has other plans for us, doesn't it?"

"Isn't that the truth?" Lucinda retorted. "The bastard takes it all away and we're supposed to accept it."

She turned on her heel and head held high, went into the house.

Alan remained by the fence in thought. Her past could have been a hard one, but he was hard-pressed to think it could be worse than his.

When he entered the house with the first trunk, only Elma greeted him. She directed they be placed in Mr. Hawkins' old bedroom, and Alan took them there, until one by one all three were lined up against the wall. Each time he passed, he stole a glance into the front room where Mae and the older woman, Miss Lady sat on chairs drinking coffee and chatting amiably.

And although in the same room, Lucinda appeared to be miles away. Standing by the large window, she peered out at the horizon. By the forlorn expression on her face, he wondered if she'd rather be back outside.

Chapter Twenty-Two

WITH MAE DISTRACTED by Miss Lady's visit, John was able to steal away and go to town. His money finally transferred to the town's bank, he was able to move forward with the purchase of a land and a new home for himself and Wesley.

It was interesting and infuriating that the further he went from her, the harder it became to breathe. She'd become a vital part of him and didn't it just make him wonder at his decision to move away. It was for the best, it had to be. Although not sure how he felt about taking Wesley away from Mae, he needed to do this.

The time had come to make a life for himself, to find out who exactly he was meant to be. The one driving factor for him was his son. To leave a legacy for Wesley would drive him to succeed. If nothing else, losing his leg brought a realization. Life could turn without notice or reason. He would die one day, and Wesley would have something to be proud of, land and property of his own.

John rode onto the property, the entire time keeping an accessing eye on the surroundings. Lasitor pranced with impatience at the slow pace he was forced to keep.

The good-sized log cabin in the center of the property was solidly built. He dismounted and walked onto the front porch stretched across the entire front length of the building with a lone chair on it.

An owl screeched and flew past John's head when he walked through empty house he intended to purchase. The large bird flew through a broken window with one last sound of protest at being rousted.

The front room was large, with enough space for a large table and chairs. On the opposite side was a sturdy fireplace with a hook and lever installed to hold a cast-iron pot to be used for heating water. An iron stove remained opposite with several sturdy shelves on the wall next to it.

John opened a door to a smaller room, which was probably used as a larder once and mouse scurried across his boot for shelter. He looked back towards the window. The owl certainly must have stayed well-fed, buy the looks of it.

Upon entering another room, which stored a few pieces of furniture, he lifted a canvas and began to sneeze as a cloud of dust filled the room. There was a great deal of work to be done, and he wondered if it wouldn't be easier to empty it completely and begin anew.

All together, the house consisted of three good-sized rooms, a kitchen living area, and two bedrooms. It would be more than enough for Wesley and him.

He went to the front and pictured a table surrounded by not only him and Wesley, but also a woman. The woman of course was Mae, and he bit back a curse and went to the front door and yanked it open.

John scanned the horizon. The land was flat, but green. A fence in dire need of repair attempted to encircle a space large enough to use for holding horses. A barn would have to be built. According to the banker, there was a natural spring on the land, not too far from the house, that would provide drinking water for the house and the animals.

It was perfect for him.

Yet the heaviness in his chest kept him from returning to town to make a final offer. He'd told the banker he'd return in a day with one, but he found his gaze going in the direction of Hawkins' ranch. It was only two hours ride from where this house was, but it may as well be a hundred. Once he left, it would change everything.

The last two days he'd only seen Mae at dinner as she'd kept busy with Miss Lady. He'd spent the time with Alan, ensuring everything was in order so he could remain as foreman without too much work since he planned to hire the ranch hands to come help him get this land ready.

Horses neighed in the distance, and John shaded his eyes with his hand to get a better look. Two men rode toward the house. It seemed the banker would not wait for him to come to town.

The man came to meet him and collect payment.

Chapter Twenty-Three

"IS SOMETHING BOTHERING you Mae? I don't think you've heard a word I've said in the last few minutes." Joshua was a perceptive man it seemed. Especially since she tried hard to remain interested in the man's explanation of what needed to be done in order to have enough manpower to prepare the land for winter within the following month.

Her thoughts centered on the stark fact. John was gone. His absence left an empty space in her life, and as much as she tried to push it away, his departure remained forefront in her mind constantly.

"No Joshua, I'm sorry I find myself preoccupied. I apologize. I agree that Alan should go into town and hire a man to help in the stables, but just to be safe, please ensure that he speak to the sheriff. There are only women here alone during most of the day, when he and the field hands are out working. Even the new stable hand will be out of earshot in the stable with the horses. And more men to help with the land are needed as well."

His hazel gaze met hers, with a smile, and she fought not to look away. "Yes ma'am."

It did not escape her attention Joshua was an attractive

man, the graying at his temples and slight creases on the corners of his eyes from days out in the sun gave him a weathered strong appearance. His large hand swept his sandy brown hair out of his face, and he took a breath. "Listen Mae, I would like to ask you something on a more personal level." His gaze slid to her face and then away. "I'd like to ask if you'd like to join me on the ride into town, and perhaps we can have a meal there."

Oh God.

"I'd love to, but with Miss Lady here and me having to take Wesley to see his father…" Mae studied the man and could only see kindness. Perhaps it was time for not just John to move on.

"Soon then?" He prompted and Mae relented.

"Yes. I would like that."

"WHAT DO YOU think Miss Lady?" Mae asked once again later in the day and blew into her hot tea. "I don't know how I feel about accepting his invitation. I mean he is kin. Well sort of."

Instead of replying Miss Lady looked to Elma who replied. "Senor Joshua is a good man. Senora Mary and Senor Joe doted on him. After his parents died one after the other from illness, they raised him as their own and he repaid them by always remaining an obedient boy and later the good man he is today."

Elma's knowing gaze lingered on hers. "He will make someone a good husband one day."

"But?" Mae prompted already knowing what Elma's reservations were.

"He deserves a woman's full heart."

Mae nodded in agreement. "Yes, he does."

Elma picked up the sleepy Wesley and left hushing him when he began to wake. Mae's gaze followed the pair, and she smiled when Wesley promptly fell back to sleep.

"Your heart will break when he goes to live with his father. You may as well prepare yourself and be strong." Miss Lady's soft smile went from the child to her. "As far as the man, Joshua, goes, don't get his hopes up. It won't be fair to him, although…"

"Of course Miss Lady, you're right. I will talk to him in the morning and tell him I cannot go into town."

Miss Lady placed her hand over hers and stopped her ranting. "It's not what I'm tellin' you girl. What I was sayin' is that it wouldn't be fair to him, if you're going to continue to expect for something with Captain McClain. Although Joshua Hawkins is a handsome man and may be just want you need to get Captain McClain out of your heart, you need to make sure first."

"Oh goodness, I don't know what to think. It's too soon. I need time." Mae slumped forward.

"Now," Miss Lady began again. "When you take the child to see his daddy tomorrow, make sure you keep your distance. A lady does not lead on two men at once."

A chuckle escaped, and Mae shook her head. "Miss Lady, I am not leading anyone, anywhere."

SPRING WAS IN full bloom; the fields were lush and green. From her bench seat the beauty of the land did not escape Mae's notice as she rode alongside Alan toward John's house. Wesley leaned against her, seated between them in his hands a wooden horse his father had made for him.

"The gray mare is about to foal any day now, very late for it, but I suppose nature has its way not carin'." Alan told her, Mae suspected he spoke just to make conversation.

Mae nodded. "It seems early. Did Joshua speak to you about hiring men to prepare the land?"

"Yes. He's just hired two field hands in town. Said there were plenty of colored men looking for jobs, told me where to find them."

"I can go with you."

"No ma'am, he suggested I go alone as it's not the kind of area to bring a lady along to." His eyes went to her briefly. "I will go in the next few days. Don't fret about it."

They arrived at John's farmhouse. From the looks of the building, John had completed much work on it. New front porch steps were built and a fresh shed attached to the side. Alan helped Wesley down and then her.

The boy ran towards the house just as John walked out. He wiped his hands on a cloth and took the boy into his arms. Over the child's head, John looked to her. Mae's stomach pitched at seeing him. He appeared sturdier, tanned. At first he did not acknowledge them, but his gray gaze locked on Alan when the man went to help her down. Mae noted his lips thinned.

"I made you some new toys," John told Wesley and placed

a kiss on top of the now squirming child's head.

With a happy yelp, Wesley raced into the house.

Mae reached for a basket from under the bench while Alan went to the back and unloaded some bags of feed and seed, which Mae brought as a gift for John. Her footfalls echoed up her body with each step toward the porch. She made her way to John who finally stepped down to meet her.

"It's nice to see you Mae." From his stoic expression she had a hard time believing it. "What is he unloading?" He looked to Alan who unloaded the last sack.

With a shrug, she went into the house not waiting for him to help her with the basket. "A housewarming gift."

His uneven footsteps followed her inside.

Once inside, she placed the basket on a large table, which looked to be newly constructed, and Mae ran her hand over the top of it. "This is beautiful. Did you make it?"

"Yes." The warm breath on the back of her neck made her close her eyes, but she stepped away and turned toward Wesley who'd already claimed his toys from a basket beside the hearth and began to set up an elaborate display.

Her eyes scanned the room. "The changes in here are unbelievable." She smiled at John, but then caught sight of Alan in the doorway.

"Would you like me to move those sacks into the shack?" Alan asked John who also turned to him. "It may rain this afternoon. Won't do to leave them out there."

"I'll come help," John replied. Then giving her a lingering look, he left to go with the man.

Mae collapsed onto a chair. Why did just John's presence

alone have her second-guessing her decision to accept spending time with Joshua? Her heart beat so hard it banged against her breast. Was this what a cheater felt?

John had all but told her to move on. He had no intention of seeking a relationship with her. So why did she feel guilty about considering a relationship with Joshua? Her palm hit the table, and she growled under her breath.

"Miss Mae?" Alan beckoned her from the doorway, and she got up and went to him. They walked to the cart and he stopped, placing one hand on the side of the wagon. "I'll go see about picking up the staples from the general store." He looked past her to the house and frowned. "Will you be all right? You can accompany if you wish."

The unexpected invitation took her by surprise. Not sure why she should decline, Mae could only stare at him. She stalled for time to come up with a reason not to accompany him. "I—I was not planning to go into town." She smoothed her hands down her skirt and Alan's lips curved knowingly.

"Not dressed for town Miss Mae?" His eyes twinkled when meeting hers and Mae smiled up at him with gratitude. "Very well, I will leave the wagon and go into town on horseback. I have the large saddlebags with enough space to hold the supplies you need."

"Thank you Alan." Mae watched him mount and realized she genuinely liked the man.

"You're welcome Mae," Alan replied and touched the tip of his hat.

Mae made it back to the house just as John came from the side of the shack. He lifted his hand at Alan who rode past him toward town.

They entered the room, and John moved toward Wesley and leaned to inspect the child's toys. "You're got quite a set up there Wesley."

The boy gave him a proud smile and continued to play.

Mae sat at the kitchen table and reached for the embroidery she'd brought along to keep busy with. John approached her and peered down at her. "I have to finish checking the fencing to make sure the horses don't get out."

She looked to him and forced a bland expression. "Go on John. I know you have things to do, so I will keep Wesley company. You can spend time with him once you finish."

Two hours later, Mae called both to John and Wesley, who sat together to the table, and father and son went to wash up.

Mae carried the steaming pot to the table where Wesley and John were already settling into chairs. Matching pairs of eyes followed the ladle to the bowls and she held back a chuckle. "John can you please pull the bread from the basket."

The three ate keeping the discussion light to include Wesley who managed to eat almost as much as the adults. Mae quizzed the boy on his words to show John how much progress he'd made?

Soon they finished eating and Mae allowed John to pour her coffee while Wesley went back to play.

"I've inquired about a housekeeper, and Mrs. Shelby, the seamstress in town recommended a widowed woman who's looking to do such a thing. I will go see about meeting with her next week."

"There's certainly no hurry…" Mae began.

"Yes there is," John interrupted her. "Its time for my boy to live here. I appreciate all you've done and continue to do for us."

"But?"

"I could never repay you for everything. By the way, thank you for the feed. I planned to go into town to get more." His lips curved and she was mesmerized at the sight. "Your bottom lip is quivering. Please tell me it doesn't mean you are about to cry. Mae, you do this each time I talk about bringing Wesley home to live with me." The concern in his eyes made her want to cry even more.

"Home?" She swung away from him and blinked away the moisture. "I am not about to cry John. There is something in my eye. You're right I'm sorry. He is your son and should be with you. It's just that I will miss his so."

"Thank you for loving my son," John moved to stand in front of her, his eyes concentrating on the cloth napkin she wrung with both hands.

Mae closed her eyes. She would not cry, had to be strong. After all, John had a right to have his son living with him.

"It seems Joshua is interested in courting you."

John's flat statement shook her, and Mae swallowed. Deciding it was best not to respond, she got up to clear the table. John's hand over hers stayed her.

"Your lack of reply tells me that perhaps I'm right." Although the words were spoken in a soft tone, she heard the anger that bubbled beneath the calm façade and was secretly gratified by it.

"My lack of reply is just that John. I don't have anything to say about Joshua to you. What does or does not happen between us is just that, between us." She slid her hand free and picked up the bowls.

John stood and followed her. "I miss you Mae. I…"

Her skirts swished around her ankles when she swung to John. "Don't John. Don't you dare say things to me that will do more than merely confuse me. Words that, once spoken, will not make me feel any better."

When his gaze swept from her eyes to her lips Mae looked toward Wesley who'd now fallen asleep in front of the fire, a wooden horse clutched in his chubby hand.

Her breathing hitched when John's lips touched hers, and she savored the feel of them as the kiss became harder, stronger. His hands slid up her arms, the skidding of his fingertips leaving a heated trail on her skin. Mae held onto his wide shoulders and kissed John back. Hoping to memorize the feel of each press and nip Mae gave in to the moment, the feel of him the taste of John McClain.

"No." She pushed away, but could not move too far as she was against the dry sink. "This is not right."

"Why? Because you're in love with Joshua?" John's bright eyes darted to Wesley who'd not budged, then back to her. "Is that it Mae?"

"Yes John, that's right. I fall in love with a different man every season. Wait until summer, perhaps it will be Alan." She pushed him aside and stormed to the doorway and peered out.

"Don't try to change my words." John came to stand beside her.

"Don't try to make me feel guilty for moving on," Mae

snapped, and she glared at him. "It's not fair."

"Then it's true. You are making a go of it with Joshua." He watched her for a few moments before raking his hand through his hair. "I suppose it's to be expected. A beautiful woman like you is a treasure."

Mae rolled her eyes and watched the horizon. As soon as Wesley woke, it was time to leave. "Never took you for a poet McClain."

"How do you feel about me?" John took her shoulders and held her still, his eyes boring into hers.

"What?" Mae could only gawk back at him. "I can't answer that right now. Why would you ask me that John?"

This time the kiss was soft and brief. His chest moved with his faster breathing when he straightened, dropping his hands to his sides. "Answer the question Mae."

"Give me a reason for your question? Tell me why should I reconsider a relationship with Joshua?" She looked into his eyes, but could not make out anything from the flat expression.

Eyes locked with hers, he let out a deep breath looking as if in pain. "You're right. I cannot offer you anything Mae."

"So you say. It's time for me to go." Mae went around him to fetch the sleeping child.

"I HUNGRY," WESLEY announced upon waking. Bundled next to her, the child wiped his eyes and looked up at her. Just the sight of the gray eyes so alike his fathers made her stomach pitch.

"Here sweetie." Mae handed the boy a piece of leftover

bread she'd saved for him. "We're almost home."

Home. Soon it would not be his home. He'd go live with John, and the other half of her heart would be taken from her.

Chapter Twenty-Four

A LAN SPOTTED LUCINDA Roberts by the same fence, this time dressed in a bright yellow dress. Like a ray of sunshine against the backdrop of the cloudy skies, trees and pasture she stood with her head cocked to the side and studied the horizon, not seeming to see what was before her at all. Whatever weighed heavily on her mind kept her from noticing him until he was but a scant foot from her.

Her eyes immediately narrowed and her full lips thinned as she considered him. "It's not polite to sneak up on a person Mister Murphy," she told him speaking down her nose. "But I suppose manners are not adhered to here in the west."

"Miss Roberts." Alan tipped his hat. "Seems the fresh air is not to your liking."

"True, I'd rather not be here." She replied taking a step away from him. "There is nothing here for me."

"You haven't given it a chance."

"I've been to Texas before. It was not a welcoming place. I hate it."

"Experiences do have a way of changing a place for us don't they?"

Lucinda huffed and picked up her skirts. "Please don't

attempt to act as if you understand me."

"Excuse me?" Anger simmered and Alan stared at the frustrating woman. "I am attempting to hold a conversation with you Luciana. Trying to understand you. That's all."

Her nostrils flared, her eyes snapped to his. "I'm not sure you could ever understand me Mister Murphy."

"You do seem to possess a large share of bitterness and self-pity, so perhaps you're correct Miss Roberts." When her eyes widened and her mouth opened, he rounded her and stalked towards the bunkhouse. Thank God the other ranch hands did not live there. At the moment he needed privacy.

Just as Alan reached the doorway, he could not help but look back to where Lucinda Roberts stood. She remained stock still, her hands to her sides, her face downward. Perhaps he'd been too harsh. The thought of returning and apologizing struck him, but his pride stopped him from going to her. Seeming to sense his regard, she lifted her face and look toward him.

Sorrow was etched across her beautiful face; but the instant she noticed he saw her, she yanked up her skirts and swung away running to the large house.

The dim interior of the bunkhouse soothed him. Alan walked past the four neatly made beds on both sides of the large room to the end where he pulled one of the chairs away from the square wooden table and sat. He focused on the chest along the far wall where he kept the few belongings he'd kept when moving to Hawkins' ranch.

Along with his shirts and trousers, there was a small framed picture of his wife and two boys. How wrong Lucinda was to think she was the only one with a right to be bitter and angry. A man could succumb to a life of drink and sorrow; he knew it more than most having spent two years after their deaths in such a way. But he'd woken up one day with the conviction that although he'd lost his family to diphtheria, he'd be doing them a disservice by not being the husband and father they'd loved. The same morning he made a decision that he would live a good life to pay them honor.

Chapter Twenty-Five

ONCE THEY ARRIVED back at Hawkins ranch, Mae turned Wesley over to Elma and rushed to her bedroom.

Collapsing on the bed, she fought to bring her breathing under control. After several long shaky breaths, she closed her eyes and put her face in her hands.

Joshua waited for her in the front room, and she had to face him. Spend time with him.

She splashed water on her face and brushed the windblown strands into a semblance of order. After she assessed her appearance, Mae went to the front room.

Joshua stood when she entered, his shy smile warmed her. And when he reached for her elbow to assist her to sit, she found herself faltering.

He shook his head. "It's strange. I grew up in this house, but it looks so different since you've moved into it. It's brighter or something. I feel more like a guest when I am in this room."

While he looked around, Mae studied him. He was pleasant, about the same height as John, but with a more husky build. She wondered why he'd not married. "Why have you not married Joshua?"

He shrugged. "I've been so busy with my lands and helping

Uncle Joe out the last few years. It's rare I have time to venture into town. If you notice, there aren't many women out here."

"I can see that." Mae replied with a smile.

"More surprising to me is you not married already."

The time to divulge why she'd remained single. The words began to form and her heartbeat quickened. "I'm not the type of woman respectable men marry Joshua. You see my business back in Virginia is not reputable. Miss Lady and I run a brothel. I am a madam."

Other than a slight frown and cock of his head to the side, Joshua did not seemed at all perturbed by her revelation. "It's strange I never considered what your business was. Not until Miss Lady and Lucinda arrived. The younger woman with her bright clothing and walk made me wonder."

"Well now you understand why I remain single." Mae looked at him relieved at the lack of judgment in his regard of her.

"What you just told me changes nothing." A slight curve of his lips took her attention. "I would like to get to know you better Mae." He hesitated. "I hope I'm not being too forward, as I don't know the nature of your relationship with John McClain."

"He…he cannot get past my background. Perhaps the fact his men frequented my establishment has tarnished his opinion of me."

"Then he's a fool," Joshua neared and took her hand. "Allow me the opportunity. I've wanted a wife and children for so long, yet never thought it would be."

Mae met his eyes. Such kindness, he deserved a woman's

entire heart and she wasn't sure she'd ever be able to give him that. "I will consider it. Please allow me time to think about it."

Joshua raised her hand to his lips and placed a kiss on her knuckles. "I better go, have much to do. I will return on Sunday, if you permit me to accompany you to church."

After Joshua left, Mae remained seated, not sure what to think or do.

What was she doing? Could she possibly marry Joshua? She'd made it past the obstacle of disclosing to him her past and dealing with the possibility of his rejection. He'd proven to be a sensible man who approached each day with quiet acceptance.

If only John would look at her in such a manner. No matter what the man said or attempted to say, she knew the truth behind his inability to forge a relationship with her. He simply could not get past the fact she'd spent her entire life until recently in a brothel. And truth be told, it was for the best. If they'd stayed together, she would be forced to live with the constant shadow of his disapproval, and after years, it would be exhausting.

A husband, now she found herself in need of one. The thought made her chuckle. In Virginia she could remain without a partner, live out her life in the large white house in the outskirts of town. But here in Texas, a woman needed a man. Protection was as much a need as the air in the still untamed part of the country, and she should marry if she was to remain.

She'd speak to Joshua and forge an agreement to marry once they got to know each other better. She'd force John from her heart.

The decision was made. She'd remain in Texas. To be far from Wesley was no longer an option. Her already broken heart would crumble to a thousand pieces if she could not see him. That alone would fortify her strength to remove John McClain from her heart.

Joshua had alluded to other children. Yes, she'd have a family and love them, but Wesley would remain imbedded in her heart, to not be displaced by any other child.

She touched her lips and thought about the hunger in John's kiss. From now on she'd avoid being alone with him. Until John hired the caregiver, she'd send him to visit his father with Alan and Elma.

It was only fair if she agreed to marry Joshua that she give him the respect due a husband. Mae lowered to her knees and bent her head in prayer. "God please take John out of my heart. Replace the deep love I have for him with love for you and my future husband. I want to be a good wife. Take this piercing pain away each time I think of John." A single tear slid down her cheek unabated.

A knock on the door followed by Miss Lady's voice brought her to the present. "Come join me for tea girl. We haven't talked about your plans for the house in Virginia."

"I'll be right there Miss Lady," Mae replied forcing a light tone.

Chapter Twenty-Six

ALAN TRIED TO hide a smile at Lucinda's attempts to keep as wide a distance between them as possible on the bench of the wagon. With Miss Lady and Elma on the back seat, she'd had little choice of where to sit. He slid his gaze to her and cocked an eyebrow. "You could ride in the very back, I'm sure the bouncing would be minimal at this pace."

Narrowed eyes met his. "No doubt you'd pick up the pace once I was back there."

"You have a bad opinion of me Miss Roberts." Alan replied his attention on the horses.

Lucinda sniffed. "I'm sure my opinion matters very little to you."

This time he faced her, not looking away until her eyes lifted to his. "It does matter. Very much."

As if to ensure the women in the back could not overhear them, she looked to them. Their conversation never stopped, and her shoulders lowered. "You enjoy shocking me Mr. Murphy, do you not?"

"Call me Alan." The only reply was a tightening of her lips.

Once they arrived at the chapel, Alan climbed down and began to help the ladies down. Arms entwined, Elma and Miss

Lady made their way to the entrance. Last down from her perch, Lucinda seemed more than reluctant to go inside. With a grim expression, eyebrows drawn and lips pulled tight, she stood without moving.

"I will sit with you and ensure you're all right," Alan told her, not quite sure why the need to protect her came over him. "Come on Miss Roberts." He held out his arm and was shocked silent when she slipped her arm through.

LUCINDA'S HEARTBEAT QUICKENED. Why had she agreed to come today? The closer they got to the entrance of the church, the larger the urge to flee became and her breathing hitched. She and God had a huge misunderstanding, and there was still too much anger in her to step inside the church and pretend all was well. It would be a lie to allude to him she did not hold a grudge at his allowing her husband and son to die in front of her eyes.

Alan's arm was firm, solid, and she dug her fingers into his muscle. At the steps, she stopped walking, her eyes glued to the open doors. "I can't. This was a mistake." Lucinda took a step backward, never pulling her hand from Alan's arm. Truth be told, she feaed her legs would give out and she'd fall. "I'll wait over there by those trees," Lucinda told Alan, pushing away from him. The fact that his chest was firm under her hands did not escape her notice.

Blue eyes met hers before flicking over to where she motioned. "Why don't you just come with me? I have something to check on. We'll be back by the time service ends."

Not quite sure of anything other than she needed to get away, she allowed the man to guide her back to the wagon. He helped her onto the bench and ran toward the church doorway. After speaking to someone, he returned and climbed onto the bench next to her.

Alan Murphy was a handsome man. With sandy brown wavy hair touching his collar, broad shoulders and a slender waist, Lucinda wondered why he was not married. Unless he was, but she'd just assumed he wasn't.

The horses followed a long dirt road. In the distance she spied a small cabin and barn. A well-kept fence around the surrounding land did not pen any animals. As they neared, she realized the house was either abandoned or the owners were not there as there barn doors were flung open and no animals seemed to be inside.

"Why are we here?" Did he plan to ask her to provide a service? Lucinda stiffened. Of course she'd told him her past, so she shouldn't be surprised.

"This is my house," He replied removing his hat and scanning over the small farm. "Looks like someone was in the barn not too long ago." He pulled the wagon to the side of the house, and looked up at her. "Let me ensure all is safe before I help you down."

Lucinda nodded and eyed the reins. She should leave, return to town and leave him here. She'd not have relations with him, not that she thought herself too good for it. It was the fact she'd come to expect more from Alan for some unexplainable reason. When she leaned to retrieve the leather straps, she saw

Alan draw his gun and step into the barn. What if he was hurt?

At the thought, she scampered down from the wagon and went toward the barn. Not hearing a sound, she slowly peered from the doorway only to jump back when a plaid covered chest appeared. "Goodness Alan, you scared me to death."

A lopsided grin made her even angrier, and she stomped her foot. "It's not funny."

"It's a good thing you're beautiful when you're angry, cause you sure spend a lot of time that way." He told her walking towards the house. "Would you like to come inside?" He stretched out his hand.

It shocked her, but Lucinda trusted Alan right then, and she took his outstretched hand allowing the male to pull her towards the doorway of the house. His large framed filled the doorway, as he unlocked the door and stuck his head inside, then moving to the side he guided her inside before him. Such a gentleman, she could get used to this.

The room was of a good size, clean, recently swept and utterly empty. There was a hearth and some blankets on the floor before it, but nothing else. They walked through another two rooms, both just as empty. "Why is it empty?" She finally had to ask.

"I gave everything away, or sold it after…" He looked away from her and she finished for him.

"After your family died."

"Yes."

"Why not sell the place? Why keep it and all its sad memories?" A familiar pang began to grow in Lucinda's chest. "I would burn it to the ground." She moved away from Alan and pressed her lips together to stop talking.

"Look at me." The words more a request than a command yet she did as he bid. Her knees almost buckled at the compassion in his eyes.

Instead of bitterness or sadness, she saw warmth in his expression, on the soft curve of his lips. Not sure why, she reached up to his face and cupped his jaw with her right hand. He leaned into her touch and sighed, Alan's eyes closed for a moment. When they opened, she recognized the heat in his gaze and pulled her hand away.

Alan cleared his throat. "When I see this house, I remember the happy moments with my family. A life rich and full with love and comfort." He shook his head. "Don't get me wrong, it took me a while. For a couple of years, I did little more than exist. But then I remembered the promise my wife and I made to each other. If ever one of us left the other, we'd do everything in our power to move on. To be happy."

Abruptly pictures of her time together with William, her quite unassuming husband, appeared in the forefront of her mind. Of their whispers in the darkness of night, when they'd lay down exhausted but happy, during their trek west with their son tucked safely between them. "Promise me you'll always be content like this." He'd said one night. "I want to make you happy."

She had agreed, not knowing a few days later…

"You've left me Lucinda." Alan came back into focus.

Lucinda focused on Alan's face and realized once again how handsome the man was. Unlike William's slight build, he was tall and muscular with a square jaw and a mouth made for kissing. "Will you kiss me?"

His eyebrows shot up for a moment, and then his hands cupped her face. "Are you sure?"

Her customers were never allowed to kiss her, the one small part of her she kept for herself. For William.

She nodded, considered taking the words back until his mouth covered hers. His lips pressed against hers with hesitation, soft and tentative. His hands, on her face, he held her in place while his mouth explored her. It was…like heaven, and Lucinda did not want him to stop. Ever.

Wrapping her fingers around his shoulders, she returned the kiss and all reservations floated away. A moan escaped. She wasn't sure if it was Alan or her, but it broke the spell and both abruptly moved away.

Alan's large chest expanded and withdrew with his breathing, his lips reddened from her kiss. "I'm sorry, didn't mean to get carried away. It's been a while since…"

"Me too." Lucinda lifted her hand to touch her lips. "Should we return?"

He swallowed and moved toward her. "Yes." This time when he leaned in, he kept his hands to his sides. The kiss was sweet and chaste, yet Lucinda closed her eyes.

"I hope this means you won't be mean to me once we get back to the ranch." He smiled down at her and for the first time in a long time her lips curved in return.

"We'll see."

His laughter was rich, and she enjoyed the sound of it.

Chapter Twenty-Seven

S UNDAY MORNINGS WERE usually filled with the anticipation of attending church where Ryan Mason presided as
pastor of the newly built church. It had only been a couple of
Sundays, but they'd already formed an enjoyable routine. Mae
looked forward to seeing Patty and after service spending the
afternoon at their house sharing a meal. But today Mae was
forced to remain behind when Alan took Miss Lady, Elma and
Lucinda to church.

Although disappointed, Mae could not go and risk taking
Wesley out. He'd waken sneezing and slightly fevered, so she'd
stay home. Holding the child on her lap, she looked out the
front room's window and watched Alan leave with Miss Lady,
Lucinda and Elma toward town.

"Mama, I sick," Wesley sniffed and rubbed his hand under
his nose. Mae grabbed a cloth and wiped his face and hand.

"Yes baby, you are." She kissed his forehead relieved it was
now cooled.

She carried him to his bedroom and placed him in bed. He
promptly snuggled into the blankets and put his thumb in his
mouth. Within minutes his eyes closed and his mouth went
slack in slumber.

Mae sighed. A day alone to look forward to, she went to find her needlepoint, she'd remain inside in case Wesley needed her. Who would have thought she'd find the new hobby pleasant.

Her life was so drastically different now. Finding she enjoyed needlepoint and reading, she'd set up a place near the window in the front room where she could sew or read in the sunlight while watching Wesley pay outside and keep an eye towards the kitchen.

With her sewing basket in hand, Mae settled into the chair and pulled a throw over her lap. She picked out her current work and studied it. The design depicted a horseman looking down at a woman carrying a basket. A pang jolted her at not realizing until now the scene familiarity of her first meeting with John. She pulled the needle from the fabric and began to stitch, filling the woman's dress with a pale blue thread. If she kept at it, the project would be completed today.

Mae's head snapped up at hearing a whimper from the back room. She must have nodded off while sewing and was disoriented as to the time. Another cry sounded, and she jumped to her feet allowing the sewing to fall to the floor.

Wesley.

When she rushed into the room, she found Wesley crying and clutching at his blanket, sitting up in the center of the bed. Immediately, she climbed on the bed and pulled him into her arms. "What's the matter Honey?' She kissed his damp forehead. It was a bad dream, he was fine.

Without a word the small child snuggled into her chest, his fingers wrapping around the fabric of her sleeve. He sighed and looked up at her. "I scared."

She forced a smile and hugged him closer. "I am too baby."

The sounds of Miss Lady, Lucinda and Elma returning brought a realization she'd not done anything while they were gone. Good thing they probably ate at Patty's house so she did not have to worry about the lack of dinner.

A deeper voice sounded from the front room. A male had entered the house with them. Mae wondered until hearing him speak again. Maybe it was Joshua, no doubt coming to see her and take her for a walk as they'd done the last few days. She took one of Wesley's hands and pulled him to leave the bed. "Come on sweet. Let's get you something to eat."

As soon as they entered the kitchen, she could tell something was wrong. Lucy was bent over Miss Lady holding a wet cloth to her face while Elma and Alan looked on with worried expressions.

"What happened?" Mae rushed to Miss Lady and reached for her hand. "What is wrong Miss Lady?"

Miss Lady waved her away with both hands. "I'm fine. Lucinda is overreacting as usual." She pushed her daughter's hand from her face and frowned. "If you continue to crowd me, I may pass out again."

"Pass out!" Mae looked to Alan and Elma. "Will someone tell me what happened?"

Elma answered. "Miss Lady passed out and fell while we were on the wagon. She was out for quite a while."

"Oh God," Her eyes flew to look over Miss Lady's figure and now noted the tear in her skirts and scratches along the old woman's arm.

She crouched next to Miss Lady who huffed with indignation. "Has this happened before to you?" Her eyes went to Lucinda who met her gaze head on without replying. Lucinda's lack of reply told her more than words could have.

Alan cleared his throat. "I better get going. Got to get the horses seen to. Call me if you need anything."

"Thank you," Mae replied grateful for him being there, if for any reason she did need him.

"Help me to my room," Miss Lady told no one in particular. "I'm going to lay down for a bit."

Lucinda's gaze held to her mother, but she did not move forward instead she allowed Mae to walk Miss Lady to her room. The fact the woman actually leaned into her hand worried Mae. Something was definitely wrong.

Miss Lady pushed her away once inside the bedroom. "Go on child. I'll get myself to bed and lay down for a bit. I'll be good as new by morning." She shuffled to the bed and removed her cloak folding it neatly before placing it on the foot of the bed.

"Tell me what's wrong," Mae asked not liking the quiver of fear in her belly. "I think you are sick. We should fetch the doctor." She reached for the doorjamb and wrapped her hand around it to hold her upright when a quiver of nerves in her limbs shook her.

When Miss Lady took a long time, her head bent and then finally lifted up to meet her gaze, a soft lift to her lips made Mae felt better, but then the older woman beckoned her. "Come sit down here with me."

After releasing a breath, Mae went to the bed and sat next

to the closest thing to a mother she'd ever known and immediately took her hands in hers. "Please tell me you are fine and you will be all right." She pleaded, this time her voice hitched.

"I'm doing as well as can be expected for someone my age girl. Stop looking so scared." Miss Lady lifted her hand and cupped Mae's cheek. "You're a woman now, grew up to be beautiful one too. Both inside and out."

Mae leaned to the woman's touch her eyes welling up. "Tell me."

Miss Lady huffed. "Young folk always make a big thing out of what is natural. What happens to me is part of life dear." She shook her head and looked toward the window. "And a human life is like any day, the sun rises and eventually it falls."

A shaky breath left her, and Mae pressed her lips together to keep them from quivering. She wanted to ask more questions, but afraid she'd upset the older woman, Mae only nodded.

"I've lived longer than my sisters and brother," Miss Lady told her. "It's going to be alright. I'm an old woman Mae, just past my sixty-fifth birthday. I had Lucinda so late." Miss Lady chuckled. "Can't say who was more surprised at it, me or her father." Her eyes sparkled at the memory. "At least he got to know her before dyin'."

Mae listened to the story she knew well. Lucinda's father was a Cavalryman who'd been killed when she was but five years old. "What are you not telling me Miss Lady?"

"I'm dying Mae. One of the reasons I came here was because I want to spend these days with both of you girls. The two halves of my heart. Now, now..." Miss Lady's hand smoothed Mae's hair away from her face when she gasped. "You stay calm now Maebelle Hawkins. It's gonna be all right."

"I can't believe you're comforting me. I should be the one taking care of you, ensuring you are well and not in pain." Mae jumped to her feet. "I'm sending Alan to get the doctor." She pushed Miss Lady to lie down onto the bed. "Rest. Can I get you some tea?"

Just as she reached the door a chuckle stopped her, and she swirled to face the woman who was now laughing, her eyes twinkling. "I would prefer just to take a nap. Go on girl, go see about whatever you were doing before we got home and please do not fetch a doctor, he cain't help me right now. I'm feelin' fine."

Numb Mae stumbled out of the room only to lean on the wall in the hallway as the tears began to slide down her face. The kitchen was dark when she finally made it past the hallway, the moonlight from the window giving the room a shadowy appearance. Her eyes landed on the cloaks hanging on the hooks on the sidewall. Her hand trembled when she lifted one off the hook and slipped it over her shoulders. The darkness beckoned and she opened the door and stepped outside.

A lightening bolt lit the night, and she let out a loud sob. Breaking into a run, she headed to the barn and a few minutes later, on her horse she galloped away.

A POUNDING SOUND startled John awake. Apparently he'd fallen asleep at the table. He rubbed his eyes and blinked only to jump to his feet when another sound, closer to a thump sounded at the front door. He got to his feet and leaned his ear to the door.

"John?" Mae called from the other side and he yanked the door open. A soaking wet figure fell into the room, and he grabbed her before she fell.

"Is there something wrong with Wesley?"

She shook her head and wiped without much result at the wetness on her face. "No, he's fine." Her voice shook and she began to sob.

He lifted her face to him and inspected it for any signs of injury. "What are you doing outside alone in this rainstorm?" He pulled her toward the hallway. "Let's get you out of these wet clothes." John guided her toward his bedroom. "You can find a clean shirt in there." He pointed to a wooden truck at the foot of his bed. When she slumped against him shivering, he realized she would not be able to do it on her own.

He began to peel her clothes away and then grabbed a clean cloth and began to rub her dry with quick movements the entire time straining to ignore the soft plush tantalizing curves. After he'd helped her into a clean shirt, he settled her onto a chair back in the front room and then wrapped a blanket around her. Once he was assured she was settled, he went to see about her horse.

She remained in the same place when he returned. The fire in the hearth warmed the room perfectly and his eyes were drawn to the beauty sitting wrapped in his blanket without moving, her eyes trained on the fire. He placed a pot of water to heat on the stove and then returned to her.

"What happened tonight?" John asked after sitting down next to her.

She didn't turn toward him, instead kept her eyes on the hearth. "I am returning to Virginia."

His gut clenched at her words. "What about the ranch? I thought you planned to stay on there."

"It doesn't make any sense to stay here any longer. It's no use. I'm no use to anyone." She began to cry again and when he attempted to put his arm around her but she jerked away. "I don't want your pity John. It's clear to me now. I have to stick to reality and accept I'm not meant to be happy but to live out my life at the house in Virginia. This is my reality." She waved her hand in the air and let it fall onto the blanket slumping forward.

John did not to reach for her although he ached to do so. "Something happened didn't it?"

Mae nodded, swiping tears away with the back of her hand. When she remained silent, he got up to make them coffee. When he returned with two cups and gave her one, she took a sip and began to talk again.

"Miss Lady is dying." Mae sagged and took a deep breath. "What am I to do? I can't stand it any more John." Her eyes met his and a soft smile lifted her lips. "Every person I care about is torn from me. First my parents, you, Wesley, and now Miss Lady are leaving me. I can't do this any longer. I'm finished. I give up."

Shoulders rounded, she heaved a heavy sigh and stared at a spot on the floor. When he reached for her, this time she allowed him to wrap his arms around her.

"Wesley and I are here. We're not going away." His voice was gruff at seeing the proud woman so devastated. "I'm here Mae."

"Are you really here for me John? I don't think that is true."

When she lifted her face to him, she was offering herself to him fully and he took her mouth with desperate hunger.

Her arms slipped from under the covers, and she grabbed onto him as if he were her only hope. Mae clung to him, her lips responding to his kiss with an ardor different from any time before.

Her taste stealing any resolve, John picked her up and carried her back to his bedroom, the entire time their lips fused, probing, tasting, and taking.

They fell into the bed together and he into her softness. John reveled in the lush curves against his much sturdier body and the world became lost in the heat and emotion swirling around them like smoke, enveloping them in a vice so tight, turning back became impossible.

Mae welcomed him into her body, every touch, caress and response like the clashing of their souls. The knowledge that what existed between them was unique struck him. He would never care for someone on such a deep level. He could never love someone more than the woman there with him now.

Free of clothing, John held her against him as they became one, the feel of her undoing him to the point his eyes were squeezed shut to keep from crying out and to keep from begging her not to ever leave him. He considered divulging in detail how he felt about her. No longer could he hide the fact from himself. He loved Mae and could not fathom a future without her. She moved beneath him and the climb ensued, both seeking the highest point from which to fall and crash into the waves only to drown tangled the each other's arms.

Mae cried out his name, and John held her until her shuddering stopped and while she began to float back to him. Yet he climbed still, not sure he'd survive the fall. Finally he recognized the hoarse call as his own as he fell over the cliff and into her arms.

"I MUST GO. They'll be worried." Mae was dressed in what looked like still soggy clothes and looking down at him when John opened his eyes.

Her eyes lingered on him and then followed the descent of the blankets when they slipped to his waist as he sat up. There was no mistaking the heat in her eyes, and John smiled at her. "Good morning."

For a moment she waivered and finally her lips tugged up to a reluctant smile. "Good morning John."

"Stay. I can send someone to tell them you are here. Your clothes look to be still damp."

Smile gone, she looked toward the doorway. "It's already going to be difficult enough to forget you. I must go and hopefully arrive before my absence is noted. I have to talk to Miss Lady and find out if she wishes to go back to Virginia for…" Her eyes darted back to him and he nodded understanding what she spoke of.

"I'll come with you. I'd like to see my son. Perhaps then go on to town and see about something."

Mae hesitated and neared the bed. "I shouldn't have come last night. But I am not sorry about what happened between us." With a brow lifted she seemed to expect a challenge from him.

"Nor am I," John replied and slid to the edge of the bed. He held out his hand and when she took it, he pulled her back to the bed. "Neither am I sorry for what is about to happen now."

THEY ARRIVED BACK to the ranch and upon entering the kitchen they were greeted by an array of different reactions. Elma avoided eye contact and busied herself pouring water into the coffeepot.

From the table Joshua glared at John and shifted his gaze to her, his mouth in a tight line.

Oblivious to the tension in the room, Wesley climbed from his chair and ran to John wrapping his short arms around the bottom of his legs. John lifted the boy and hugged him before directing him to sit again and finish his breakfast.

On his feet, Alan cleared his throat finding a sudden interest in the wooden flooring and grunted something about going back to work.

After touching the brim of his hat, Joshua left the house and headed outside.

Elma looked to them and began to pour two cups of coffee. "We wondered where'd you were, and I called Joshua to ask him to go search for you." She placed the cups on the table. "I didn't say anything to Miss Lady, did not want to worry her."

"You're right Elma. I'm sorry to have worried you," Mae looked over her shoulder to a departing Joshua. "I should have left a note."

John reached for her shoulder. "I'll go talk to him."

"Thank you," Mae replied, "But there is nothing that can be said. Soon enough we'll have to discuss my returning to Virginia."

"What are you talking about girl?" Miss Lady stood at the doorway. "Mae, what nonsense are you thinking about doing now?" John froze at Miss Lady's tone and looked to both women.

Lucinda, ever present at her mother's side, looked around the room perplexed, excused herself and went past them to follow after Alan.

Miss Lady sat down, and Elma placed a teakettle on the stove turning her back to them.

"I planned to talk to you and discuss your plans Miss Lady," Mae told her and sat next to her. "We can go back to Virginia together. You like it there don't you?"

"What do you think Captain McClain?" Miss Lady looked to John whose eyes shifted to her before replying.

"I think Mae should remain here."

Mae balked and stood. "It's my life, and I have decided it's best if I leave. I need to see about my horse. She stormed outside only to stop on the back porch not ready to face Joshua. Truth be told, the thought of returning to Virginia saddened her deeply and the fact surprised her. But she knew remaining in Texas meant a broken heart upon seeing John marry another and Wesley accepting the woman as his mother. She could not marry Joshua, would never love anyone else. Her heart could not withstand it. She'd rather be away and keep the memories of their time together.

Shaken, she walked around the side of the house. The sun was still low. Its rays filtered through the branches of the trees surrounding the house giving the land around them a peaceful glow. Mae moved toward the oasis, refusing to think of anything for the next moments but instead reveling on the beauty of the day, the birdsong from the tree's branches and the soft rustling of the grass under her feet.

Mae looked up past the branches toward the sky. "Why have you forgotten me?"

John caught up with Joshua who'd made it as far as the fence and waited for him when he called.

The man did not look at him with scorn or anger, more resigned than anything. "You planning to marry her? Because if you don't I'll be forced to hit you and I like you McClain. But Mae, she deserves to be cared for."

"I care for Mae. And I will marry her if she will have me." John was surprised at his own answer, but he meant each word. He felt lighter. He was finally going to allow her the opportunity to choose whether or not she'd accept him as her husband.

"Then I have to accept it." Joshua looked past him toward the house. "Funny, I never really felt things would progress between us. It's obvious she has deep feelings for you."

"I'm sorry." John told him meaning it.

Joshua shrugged. "Don't be. I want a wife and children one

day. I hope for a woman who loves me and don't want to share my wife's heart with anyone."

"I can understand," John replied and held out his hand.

The men shook hands, and Joshua walked toward his horse. "I hope to see you around McClain."

MAE ENTERED THE barn. The smell of fresh hay accompanied by the sounds of the horses welcomed her. Alan kept the area clean and organized. She'd yet to find fault with the man's work ethic. He lived in a set of rooms attached to the barn and seemed to spend every waking hour taking care of the horses, tending to the livestock or mending fences. He completed anything needing to be done quickly and efficiently without prompting and she was glad for it.

Upon spotting her mare, Mae went to the horse. The mare's head reached out toward her, and Mae ran her hand over the soft nose. "Hey girl." She reached into her pocket and pulled out an apple and held it out, which the horse gobbled up immediately.

"What can I do for you Miss Mae?" Alan was always formal and respectful, Mae noted, as the man neared.

Alan held reins in his hand and stood with an easy grace. Being outdoors had to be a natural part of him. Earlier that morning when she and John had come home was the first time she'd ever noticed him as anything but relaxed.

"I apologize for worrying you and the others."

"There is no need." Alan neared and reached towards the mare, setting upon opening the gate. He went into the stall and began to look the animal over. "I know you and McClain have something."

"He and I are not meant to be together. We are too different." She wasn't sure why she spoke the words, but something about Alan made her comfortable. Either way it didn't matter as she was leaving.

"You can't help who you love."

Mae frowned. "As I said, there is no future for us Alan. I came to talk about my leaving Texas. I am returning to Virginia, without John."

His hazel eyes lifted to hers. "You are a fool then."

Her eyes widened at his words. "I have to do what I can, what is best for me."

"Life is about sacrifice Miss Mae. It's not always easy."

The mare trembled with anticipation as he led it back out of the stall towards the corral and Mae followed them. "I *am* making a sacrifice Alan. It's going to hurt like hell to leave Wesley here in Texas. I love that boy. It's going to be terribly difficult to leave this ranch and Elma…"

He turned so fast she stumbled back a step. "Then why are you leaving? What will it solve?"

"What about you Alan?" Mae retorted. "What are you running away from? You live here alone and keep to yourself. Who did you leave behind?"

"You think that by asking me these questions you don't have to answer mine?" He released the horse into the corral and leaned on it. "I left my wife and children after I buried them. My Anna died first and the children followed. I couldn't stay in the same house so I left. But I will give love another opportunity if it presents itself."

"I'm so sorry."

He held his hand up and smiled, the action bringing forth a dimple that caught her eye. "It's all right Miss Mae. You are hurting and when it happens, it's natural to lash out. I was out of line when I spoke."

"No Alan, you are right. I am taking the easy way out. But I'm tired." She sighed. "How can you be positive?"

"I have a feeling here." He punched his gut. "That the woman I'm to be with is not that far."

Mae nodded and smiled at him. "I like you Alan."

"I care for you too Miss Mae, and that's why I hate to see you throw your chance at happiness away."

"Mae?" Lucinda appeared from the barn a basket in her hand. "Supper is ready."

Alan's eyes softened when lighting on Miss Lady's daughter. Mae motioned Alan forward. "Would you like to join us for dinner?"

A knowing smile curved her lips when the male kept his gaze downward and nodded.

"Thank you Alan." She pressed a kiss to his jawline and hurried away, leaving Lucinda and Alan to follow.

Chapter Twenty-Eight

SWEATY AND DIRTY, *Lucinda struggled from under the man's heavy arm. His bawdy laughter rung loudly in her ears when she crawled away from him. "She's all yours Henry," he said into the darkness.*

A hand grabbed around her ankle, and she was dragged in another direction. When she swung and hit the man's face, he backhanded her so hard she almost passed out. The man scrambled on top of her and chuckled. "How about spending time with me now?"

Thunder boomed, and Lucinda bolted up to sit. Tears streamed down her face, and she pushed the blankets away hoping it would help her overheated body cool down and stop pulsing non-stop. It would begin to rain soon. God, how many times did the dream have to return? Why now? It had been almost a year since she'd dreamed of her capture after William was killed.

Her skin crawled, and she left the bed. She could not sleep, not tonight. At the window, she looked toward the bunkhouse. A soft light beckoned.

"ALAN?" THE VOICE penetrated through his sleep, and Alan opened his eyes. Someone was at the door.

He got up and went to open it.

In a long white gown, Lucinda stood in the doorway, her eyes reddened; she put a trembling hand out to him. "Let me sleep with you. You can have me, do what you wish, but I don't want to be alone tonight."

"Come in." He stood aside to let her enter and ran a hand through his hair. He wanted her. He could not deny it, but not this way. Not in payment for not being alone. "Here, come lay down." Alan followed her to his narrow bed.

When she began to untie her nightgown, he stopped her hands. "How about we wait on that?"

Lucinda nodded mutely and climbed onto the bed. When he lay down, she immediately snuggled against him and placed her head on his chest. With a deep release of breath, she looked up at him. "I couldn't sleep, never can on nights like this. Night life suits me. I can sleep during the day without a problem it seems."

"Bad dreams?"

"Bad memories," Lucinda whispered.

"Want to talk about it?"

She pushed away and went to get up, but he wrapped his arms around her and held her in place. "You don't have to Luciana, but it may help, you know, to get it all out."

Her body relaxed, but her voice quivered and it shocked him when she actually began to talk. "We fed them. They sat around the campfire and ate with us. They led William away, asking him to see about their horse. He was such a good man, always wanting to be of assistance. The two of them then beat him before one shot him. I don't know which it was. I was too shocked by what was happening. When my son ran towards them, they shot him too." She began to shake, and he ran his hand up and down her back. "After the men killed them, I prepared to be next. But they kept me alive. Spent the rest of the day there. They took turns taking me over and over."

Her entire body shook as she began to sob, and Alan's heart broke for her. "Oh God, they lay there…dead. My husband and my baby, while those animals ate our food and used me."

"How did you get away?"

"At dawn the next morning, I woke up to the sound of horses. They left, just left. Took all our food and provisions."

"I'm so sorry."

Lucinda lifted her face to him. "I've never told anyone about what the men did to me. I wish they would have killed me."

Alan kissed her forehead. "You were very brave Lucinda. Those bastards will pay for what they did, sooner or later, you can trust that. Did you return home then?"

She nodded. "I dragged both my son and husband to the wagon. Somehow I found the strength and loaded their bodies onto it and road back to Virginia. It took me a long time to get back, but I needed to give them a proper burial."

In the dark silence that followed, Alan held Lucinda who let out a quiet sniffle. "I meant it when I said you can have me."

"I know you did, but it's not what I want from you Lucinda."

"What could you possible want then?" The puzzled look on her pretty face made him ache for her.

"I want to court you, get to know you better. I want to fall in love with you."

Her eyes widened, but she did not reply right away. "I think you are confused Mister Murphy." There was levity in her words, and she placed her head back on his chest. "I'm going to close my eyes for just a few minutes."

When her breathing evened out, Alan finally allowed the anger for what happened to her to be release. How could men do such terrible things to a family? It was unfathomable to him. The cruelty of what she'd been forced to endure made him want to hunt the animals down and kill them. And maybe one day the opportunity would present itself. But until then he had to hold on to the belief they'd pay for their actions.

Lucinda let out a shaky breath, and he kissed the top of her soft hair before placing his cheek to it. Alan waited for sleep to claim him as well.

Chapter Twenty-Nine

"IT'S NOT A good idea Mae. You are not thinking clearly," Patty's grim eyes scanned Mae's face as if looking for a clue to what she thought at the moment. The Jacobs' had come to visit and Mae was glad to see her friend. It gave her the chance to talk to her about her impending departure.

"I have to." Mae remained stubbornly adamant about returning to Virginia. Even after talking to Miss Lady and the woman refusing to return with her. Mae was sure she'd end up convincing her.

"What about Wesley? Surely you won't leave the child. He sees you as his mother." Patty pressed on.

"I am not his mother. The sooner I leave, the easier for him to accept whoever John marries. He told me he planned to go to town. I'm sure it's to hire Wesley's caregiver. The woman will be living with them, things will happen. I can't stand to be around to see it. Understand me Patty."

Patty slapped her hand on the tabletop and Mae jumped. "He is not marrying anyone. The man is in love with you. If only the both of you would stop being so stubborn, you'd realize you're made for each other."

"Bah!" Mae stood and went to rinse her cup. "Would you

like to go for a walk?" She looked towards the living room. "Where is Ryan?"

"He's in the barn, speaking to Alan about an unruly horse we bought. Alan is the best man to get information about breaking a horse."

"Come," Patty slipped her arm through Mae's. "Lets take advantage of this spare time. Miss Lady and Wesley are asleep."

The afternoon was brisk, a bird flew overhead and Mae watched it land in a nest and begin to feed the chicks in its nest. "It's a beautiful day. I am going to miss this. The space, the land…"

"Then don't leave," Patty finished for her. "Give it time Mae. I suggest you speak to John and ask him what his plans are, what he feels." Patty's eyes went past her. "Ah there he is now."

Mae's stomach pitched when spotting John nearing. In a worn blue shirt tucked into his pants, his wide shoulders and slim hips were emphasized. The picture of them in his bed assailed her, and Mae felt herself redden. She began to babble, her nerves taking control. "I wasn't aware he was here. I'm sure he's here to see Wesley. I shouldn't be alone with him. I can't resist his touch. I'm not strong enough."

"Well, you should remain strong against it," Patty replied lightly. "I understand the need of being with a man, but in this case, I believe it would be beneficial to wait."

"Wait?" Mae frowned. "I am never going to be with him again Patty. It's not right I understand it believe me. Plus it will only make it harder for me when I leave."

"Um hmm," Patty replied before turning to John. "Good

afternoon John. I was just about to go see where Ryan's gotten off to. I'll see you both in a little while."

John's gray eyes met Patty's briefly before going to Mae. "How are you Miss Patty?"

The woman smiled at him. "I'm well." She walked away, and neither of them spoke. Mae braced herself for whatever John was about to tell her. No doubt he'd hired someone to care for Wesley and came to inform her he came to take Wesley with him. When she felt strong enough, she met his gaze.

"Why do you seem afraid of me?" John's brows drew together. "Are you angry with me?"

"N-No, of course not," Mae stuttered. "Wesley is napping now, but he should awaken shortly. Would you like to come in for coffee?"

"I came to see you." The words vibrated through her and she took a breath. "I haven't seen you in days. The last time I came to see Wesley, only Elma was about. Then it was she and Alan who brought him to see me." He reached for her and then let his hand fall. "It seems you are avoiding me."

Mae inhaled and tore her eyes away from his darkened ones. "I find it best to keep a distance between us. You have to admit, it will make it easier once I leave."

"Easier?" He asked. "For you or for me?"

"Both of course," Mae told him and took a step back. "It's not right John. But it's hard for me to resist reaching for you when near you. My feelings are too strong, I desire you, want to touch you and be touched by you."

His breathing hitched at her words. "I feel the same way. It's what I came to talk to you about."

The rising and lowering of his chest mesmerized her and Mae could only wait breath held. Did he come to ask her to be his lover?

"I am in love with you Mae. Marry me."

Her heart stopped at the words. But what shook her was the earnest expression on his face. He waited for her to respond with ill concealed trepidation, his body tight and leaning just a bit forward.

"I can't." Mae refused to meet his eyes; instead she focused past his left shoulder to where cattle grazed. "I believe you love me. But I also know you cannot get beyond my past. It will always be hard for you."

"I've come to grips with it Mae and…"

"No you have not," Mae interrupted him. "What will happen when the first man comes along who knows about me, and everyone in town becomes aware of my past? What will you do then? Will you be able to walk beside me with you head held high?"

"The loss of my leg is what made me falter more than anything Mae. The fact is I'm the one who doesn't deserve you. I am sure you warrant a full, able-bodied man to be your husband. But the idea of anyone with you makes my blood boil. It made me realize I needed to take a chance."

Mae could only stare at him agog.

"Come with me." He took her elbow and steered her toward the house. "I will not accept no for an answer."

Soon they were riding away from the ranch on the front bench of the same wagon they'd rode from Virginia on. A stoic John beside her, Mae slid glances to him from the corner of her eye. "Where are we going?" The rambling road soon turned to a more open space and she took in the scenery. They did not head towards town but away from it and in the direction of where they'd come from so many months ago.

"Look." John pointed to a huge eagle flying overhead.

"He's beautiful," Mae replied as the bird swooped and gracefully lifted again toward the sky. "Where are you taking me John?"

"To a place where you'll accept my proposal."

"What?" She placed her hand on his arm and he faced her. Her eyes drank in his features before she could speak again. "I don't understand."

The sun was setting when they finally stopped at a familiar clearing. She climbed from the wagon and walked toward the cusp of trees near the shallow stream where they'd stopped and refreshed during their trek westbound. Without speaking, John joined her, and they walked side-by-side for a few minutes.

Mae inhaled deeply of the fresh pine air and closed her eyes imagining the day they'd been here. She didn't quite understand the significance of returning, for nothing memorable had happened here.

"The day we stopped here, we took a walk to this exact spot. You did your best to keep your distance from me, just like you are now. But I took your hand and pulled you closer beside me to walk." John voice remained even and calm and Mae found herself wondering what he'd say next.

He smiled as if reading her thoughts. "We didn't speak of much. As a matter of fact, you spent most of the time looking at flowers sprouting from between the trees. Those violet ones there." He pointed at a small crop of brilliant foliage.

Mae stepped away from him and leaned to peer at the blooms. "They are so beautiful, are they not?"

"Yes," he replied, but his eyes were on her.

Mae reached for several of the blooms and picked them. She lifted them to her face and inhaled the soft perfume. "I'm sorry, but I am not sure I remember this place; it was one of many along the way."

She looked around when noticing John's rare smile. "Unlike you, I remember it vividly because a realization came to me, and I became so angry I could barely stand it. I knew we were very close to our destination, and I pledged to leave you with your father, find Wesley and after having my leg removed, head further west. The plan was never to see you again, and I could not wait to follow through."

"I don't understand. Why were you angry?"

John took her hand and lifted it to his lips. The soft kiss on her knuckles sent a shiver down her arm. "Because I'd fallen in love with you, and I was blindsided. Surprised such a thing happened to me. I'd always been in control of my emotions, until spending time with you. No matter what I did, where I went and thought about, you were forever present foremost."

"I didn't know." Mae pulled her hand away. "Now I understand why you barely said a word when you left me at my father's ranch. Why are you telling me all this now?"

"Because you need to understand how much you mean to me. Yes I admit, I tried to fight against it, convinced myself that I could move on. But it's not true. I recognize it now." John took her hands in his and knelt before her.

"Accept me Mae. I can only offer you what I am now a man with little to offer other than my heart. I will be proud to be your husband if you allow me to be such."

Could she do it? To marry him would put not just John in danger of social disgrace, but also Wesley.

As if reading her thoughts, John reached for her other hand and looked into her eyes. "It's different here Mae. Everyone comes here to find a new life, and your past is not as important here. Say yes."

Gravity pulled her forward so that she felt as if she was about to step off a cliff to fall into the unknown, but it felt good. Freeing.

Mae nodded, and her lips lifted into a wide smile. "I love you John. I can't bear the thought of a future without you and Wesley. I've been terrified actually." She took a deep breath. "Yes, John McClain, I will marry you."

Before she could say another word, he stood and pulled her into an embrace turning in a full circle until she became dizzy. His laughter rang over the trees and hers joined it.

"Put me down," Mae laughed and then wobbled when he placed her on her feet. "Kiss me John."

His lips covered her, the kiss tentative at first, but then becoming heated when she wrapped her hands around his neck.

John's hand slid down her back, and he pulled her against him. Soon their breathing became harsher the kiss more demanding. Mae planted her palms on his chest and pushed away gently while looking up at him. "I'd like to wait until we're married before being intimate again."

He nodded and kissed the tip of her nose. "I agree."

"When would you like to plan our marriage for?" Mae took his hand and led him back toward the wagon.

"How about today?"

"Oh John." She nudged him with her elbow. "I'm serious."

"So am I."

Mae sighed, happiness engulfed her and the surrounding area seemed colorful, richer. "Why did you bring me here?"

"Because I wanted you to understand I've loved you for a long while."

"We were both heading west not knowing how much it would change our lives." Mae said.

"It was an awakening of sorts don't you think?"

Mae nodded accepting his soft kiss. "Yes John, it was."

"Let's go home and tell Wesley that his ma and pa are going to be together with him forever." John said pulling her back towards the wagon his stride long and purposeful.

"I'm not sure he's old enough to understand," Mae replied laughing.

Chapter Thirty

LUCINDA STOOD OVER her mother's grave. The emptiness in her heart so vast she felt completely hollow. Almost a month since the noble woman had passed and to Lucinda it felt as if it were just yesterday. Goodness, she wasn't sure how she'd made it past the first few days after finding Miss Lady with a peaceful expression, not waking when she'd tried to rouse her. Her mother had died in her sleep.

Thankfully, Elma was a godsend; the woman had taken care of her and Mae. Both of them in so much pain, they mourned the loss of the woman who loved them without reservations. And Alan was forever present to talk to her, walk with her, his patience seemed without bounds.

Her mother raised her and Mae to value themselves and expect the best from life. She'd failed her mother. Every night in the brothel could not have been easy on Lady Roberts, watching Lucinda sell her body, yet her mother never tried to talk her out of it. She accepted Lucinda's choices with quiet reluctance.

Now she'd lost her mother, and guilt grew heavy in knowing her mother would not live to see her start a new life here in Texas. Although she was still unsure of what she was going to do, she had plenty of money saved. Enough to start perhaps open a small boarding house for travelers. Something she noticed on their trek westward was that people were in need of places to stop and find a clean bed and a warm meal for a night or two before continuing on their travels.

"Can I walk you back?" Alan's deep voice washed over her and Lucinda allowed it to relax her.

She turned to the tall handsome man. "I haven't thanked you for the night I woke you and burdened you with my story."

The sunny day made his blue eyes appear lighter when he looked at her. "I am glad you did. And I meant what I said to you. Do you remember?"

"I do, and I treasure those words. But you deserve much better Alan. Plus, I have so much to work through. I am not sure I can let go of the bitterness just yet."

He reached forward and pushed an errant curl away from her face to tuck it behind her ear. "I don't care about your past Lucinda. And I want to help you get past all the hurt. Because when I look at you all, I see is my future."

The words shook her, and Lucinda could only stare up at him, searching his face. How could this be possible? How could it be a man like him was willing to forgive her past and accept her with such openness?

"Come walk with me," Alan told her taking her hand. They ambled for a few yards until finding a shady tree.

Lucinda leaned against the trunk and looked across the plush land toward where cows grazed, their tails swishing back and forth. "I do like it here. I'm considering purchasing a small house and opening it up to travelers."

"It would be dangerous for a woman alone," Alan told her with a frown. "Is that really what you want to do?"

"My savings will only last so long, I have to earn money and support myself."

He leaned forward and kissed her. "How about a future with me? I can provide for you Lucinda. You can move into the house, keep a garden and you can do whatever it is women do all day." He shrugged when she hit his arm and couldn't help but laugh at how men didn't seem to realize all a woman had to do in a day to keep a home.

"How about this?" Lucinda started and took one of his larger hands in both of hers. "I find I want to be with you. I think of you every morning as soon as I wake. This is new to me and I want you to be sure about it. So let's give it a few months. Plenty of time for you to get to know me, and then you can ask me again."

"I'm not going to change my mind." His eyes twinkled when he looked down at her. "But if you need time to think about it because you're scared of my handsomeness then take all the time you need."

She could only smile and shake her head. "I don't need any time. I already know I want to be with you."

"Well that's all I needed to hear." He pulled her to him and his mouth captured hers.

Miss Lady had insisted Lucinda come with her to Texas, and she'd come because she'd known something was wrong with her mother. Perhaps the true reason was that her destiny was here and it was meant to be.

For her to finally find love again in a kind and gentle Alan Murphy.

Chapter Thirty-One

"DO YOU MAE Hawkins take John McClain to be your lawful wedded husband?" Ryan stood in front of them and spoke, but all Mae could focus on were John's beautiful gray eyes glued to hers. The day had finally come when they'd be joined as husband and wife.

The wedding was all she dreamed of. The Jacobs' small chapel was replete with wildflowers and blue ribbons. Every bench filled with townspeople and friends.

The only person whose presence would have made the day even more perfect was Miss Lady. Although Mae felt her presence in her heart, it filled her and kept her smile in place.

Miss Lady would be delighted for her, for the turn of events, which she'd no doubt anticipated when forcing her on the trip west with John. Yes, Miss Lady would be sitting at the front bench with a knowing smile and happy for her in seeing she was finally joyful and fulfilled.

When it was time to exchange rings, she gave her small bouquet of blue wildflowers to Patty who stood next to her as her matron of honor. And then it was time to repeat the vows and place the golden ring onto John's finger. Her hand trembled in his, and John squeezed it to reassure her.

Wesley stood tall beside John, his face solemn when handing John her ring. Her heart swelled with pride at their little boy.

John's voice was strong when he said his vows until the last word when it hitched and she let out a breath at his being affected as much as she was.

A sniffle took her attention, and she slid her gaze over to Elma who sat next to Lucinda. Both wiped their eyes with bright white handkerchiefs and blew their noses at the same time. The Hispanic woman had been so excited at the news that Wesley would remain at the house that she'd burst into tears in the middle of the kitchen and had to be helped to sit.

Not only had Mae grown to love the child, but Wesley had managed to steal Elma and Lucinda's heart as well.

AFTER THE CEREMONY, everyone went to the Jacobs' home where a large banquet had been laid on tables outside for the celebration. Many of the townspeople were present, and Mae milled about with John getting to know the people who she'd be neighbors with now.

John's parents had traveled from Virginia for the wedding, and much to her delight, she and his mother Elizabeth McClain had immediately hit it off. Her new mother-in-law was a strong no-nonsense type who did not mince words. Just like her son, she went straight to the point when speaking. She'd taken Mae aside and told her she approved of the marriage and was glad John was marrying a strong woman and not some simpering wallflower. Mae had laughed and hugged the woman.

John's father Robert McClain was the complete opposite of her mother-in-law and son. Easy-going and patient, the man spent hours reading to Wesley and telling him stories. He'd walked to the barn and helped Alan with the care of the horses and milking of cows. The elder McClain proclaimed to fall in love with the lands and that upon news of a second grandchild, they'd move to Texas and live in John's now empty house.

His mother shook her head in response. "We'll have to split our time since the girls remain in Virginia Robert."

THE EVENING FINALLY came, and John ushered Mae into the master bedroom they would now share. Her entire body trembled in anticipation, and she fumbled with her hairpiece. Mae stood in the middle of the room waiting for him to lock the door. Everyone was abed, and the house was quiet.

John came to her and cupped her face taking her lips with his. "It's been so hard to wait until this night. It seemed like it would never arrive." He kissed her again and she squirmed attempting to unbutton his shirt.

"It will be worth it," Mae replied and caressed his face. "And because we have the rest of our lives to be together, each time will be special."

"Yes, the rest of our life." John pressed his lips to hers.

When he fumbled with the buttons down the front of her dress, she finally lost her patience. "Let's take our own clothes off," she told him, her words breathless while making quick work of the fastenings of her dress. "Hurry, John."

The crooked smile as he undressed made it harder for to Mae remove her clothing. Her heartbeat quickened as more of his body was revealed. When his shirt slipped from his wide shoulders displaying the broad expanse of chest for her eyes to feast upon, Mae stopped moving and just stared at him transfixed. His body was perfect.

Hands on his pants front, John began to push them from his narrow hips. Darkened eyes met hers. "Take your clothes off Mae." The huskiness of his request prompted her to move.

Within moments, her dress was folded over a chair, her hairpiece and short gloves next to it on the top of a table. For a strange reason, she felt shyness overtake until she lifted her gaze to John's. His eyes traveled over her body, and his chest expanded with his rapid breathing. She rushed to him.

Finally without the impediment of clothing, they clasped onto each other, mouths and bodies fused, fitting perfectly.

Mae slid her hands up his wide back and wrapped her arms around his nape. When his mouth covered hers, she pushed into him needing to touch every inch of his large body against her own.

John guided her to the bed and laid her upon it following after her.

Making love with her husband was an experience unlike anything she expected. Every moment of exploration and discovery was like unwrapping a beautiful gift. She'd never forget this night, a dream come true of being held and loved by the man she loved.

"What are you thinking Mae?" Joined with her, John stopped moving and pressed a kiss to her brow. "Why are you frowning?"

"I'm puzzled at how I could ever deserve to be so happy." Mae replied kissing his lips.

"You deserve so much more." He continued to keep an eye on her, a soft curve to his lips. "I love you."

"And I love you John McClain. But…"

"But?"

"Please keep moving; don't stop." She lifted her hips to emphasize her words.

Thankfully he took instruction well.

When their movements reached a frantic pace from which there was only one outcome, the breathtaking destination of bliss, Mae called out his name and lost all control flaying under him.

John's hoarse cry penetrated through the fogginess and she held him until he finally relaxed.

"I love you Mae, I love you so much." John began pressing kisses all over her face and Mae knew it was true because she accepted it fully, the words sinking into her very soul.

Epilogue

S ITTING ON THE front porch while he worked oil into the leather of a new saddle, John watched Mae and Wesley stroll back to the house. They'd kept their tradition of taking walks every day. Side-by-side the two loves of his life walked toward him. Mae seemed to be speaking to the boy while he listened intently. She gave Wesley lessons daily, from the basics like writing and arithmetic to history and other things. It worked out well that thanks to Miss Lady's insistence, Mae was well schooled. Wesley would grow up to be the same.

Each day John became more grateful for the beautiful woman he'd married. Now as she grew round with their second child, she insisted they refer to the baby as, claiming Wesley as her first, she was radiant.

Mae looked up and waved toward him. When their eyes met, his heart began to pound in his chest. The love he felt for her barely containable beneath his breast.

"You should not be moving around so much," John admonished when they reached the house's porch.

Mae rolled her eyes and accepted his help to sit. Elma materialized and brought with her a light blanket. "Senora Mae, you should rest. The baby will come any day now."

"If I left it up to you two, I'd spend my days in bed bored to death," Mae fussed, but accepted the blanket and placed it over her lap.

"Pa I go see the calf?" Wesley asked shuffling from one foot to the other with impatience. At almost four now, he'd began to shed his chubbiness. "Mr. Alan said I can help him."

John nodded and Wesley shot from the porch, sprinting toward the barn.

"I'm glad Alan remains with us. Wesley adores him," Mae said smiling and tracking Wesley's retreating figure.

John agreed. "Yeah, he's got a way with kids. I'm surprised he's not married and had some of his own."

Mae rolled her eyes. "Oh it's obvious, it won't be long until we celebrate another wedding and perhaps there will even be children of his running about."

"What are you talking about Mae?" John asked.

"The reason Alan remains here is the same reason Lucinda does. They care for each other, but they are taking their time, getting to know each other."

"Oh." John was glad Lucinda asked to remain when Miss Lady passed away. The solemn young woman claimed to have no reason to return to Virginia, especially since Mae sold the brothel to Butch Mason. "Now that I think about it, I have noticed certain looks between them. Heck I thought it was this land the reason they remain, everyone just falls in love with it."

She reached for John's hand and looked to the distance. "This place is beautiful, I can't wait to fill it with children, to see them run and play with Wesley and this one." She patted her stomach.

"Fill it?" John's eyebrows were raised and his mouth open in mock horror. "Where do you get the idea I want more children Missus McClain?"

Mae slapped at his arm. "I overheard you telling Joshua the other day. You've always wanted a large family."

His eyes lingered on her stomach for a moment. "I am looking forward to my life with you Mae. I love you more than life itself."

Tears sprung and she went to wipe them away but John leaned forward and took her face in his hands and kissed them away.

"I would have never taken you for such a romantic," Mae sniffed. "You were always so stern and rigid."

"Survival. It's how I could cope with everything I saw and had to do," He kissed her again softly.

"Oh!" Mae straightened and grabbed at her stomach. "That was a hard one."

John paled and stood. "Is it time?"

Mae's laughter ringed brightly. "No, the baby kicked me."

"I can't wait to spend time with our children and the Jacobs', the children become close friends. I just know it."

At the familiar speech, John kissed her brow. "It's amazing how they are expecting their first child just a few months after us isn't it?"

"It's another of many miracles in our life," Mae agreed and jumped. "Ooh another kick."

HILDIE McQUEEN

THREE DAYS LATER, John held his new daughter in his arms while sitting in a rocking chair he'd made for Mae. Moonlight from the window fell over his sleeping wife's face. Her golden hair spread over the pillow, lovely in her sleep, a soft curve to her lips, she was like he imagined angels looked like.

The baby squirmed and let out a soft whimper and even though it was a low sound Mae's eyes popped open and she looked to him. "Is Lady hungry?"

John smiled at her sudden alertness. "No she's gone back to sleep. And you should too, you need to rest."

Mae's soft emerald eyes met his and her lips curved into a slow smile. "I want to hold her. She's so beautiful. Looks so much like you. You make beautiful babies John McClain."

Warmth filled him and he got up and laid the child in her arms and then he climbed onto the bed next to his wife taking them both into his arms. "I will have to argue the point." John kissed Mae's hair. "Although her hair is dark like mine, her little upturned nose is much more like yours."

"Hmm, perhaps, but her eyes are a light blue. They will darken to a beautiful gray." Mae told him with a lazy smile.

"Is Lady 'wake?" Wesley's head appeared from the opening in the doorway. His eyes locked directly onto his sister. "Can I hold her?"

Mae shifted and gave the sleeping baby to John, and then she held her arms out. "Come here Wesley."

The boy giggled and jumped into the bed immediately snuggling into Mae's embrace. "It's hot in here Mama." He told her but John noted he didn't move away.

Mae sighed and kissed Wesley's face. "I love you so much

249

my little boy."

"I the big brother." His son replied, his voice filled with pride.

"That's true you are," Mae told him.

John reached and tussled the boy's hair.

Each day that passed since marrying Mae, he'd been thankful for the gift of a family. The blessing of a strong brave wife and a life like one he'd never imagined.

OTHER WORKS BY HILDIE MCQUEEN
(In reading order)

Where The Four Winds Collide
Colter Valley
Patrick's Proposal

BRIDES FOR ALL SEASONS – MONTANA
Wilhelmina, A Winter Bride
Aurora, A Romantic Bride
Lucille, A Lucky Bride
Esther, An Easter Bride
Scarlett, A Summer Bride

BRIDES FOR ALL SEASONS – WYOMING
Sarah, A Festive Bride
Christina, A Bride for Christmas
Amelia, An Autumn Bride

ABOUT THE AUTHOR

Being a full-time writer is no joke, the co-workers are dogs, no one cleans the office and the only human contact is usually carrying a package and in a hurry to leave.

USA Today Bestselling author Hildie McQueen loves unusual situations and getting into interesting adventures, which is what her characters do as well. She writes romance because she is in love with love! Author of western historical and contemporary, as well as some highlander romances, she writes something every reader can enjoy.

Most days Hildie McQueen can be found in her overly tight leggings and green hoodie, holding a cup of tea while stalking the lawn guy. In the afternoons she browses the Internet for semi-nude men to post on Facebook.

Hildie's favorite past-times are romance conventions, traveling, shopping and reading.

She resides in beautiful small town Georgia with her super-hero husband Kurt and three little dogs.

Visit her website at
www.hildiemcqueen.com

Facebook:
facebook.com/HildieMcQueen

Twitter:
twitter.com/HildieMcQueen

Instagram
instagram.com/hildiemcqueenwriter

Printed in Great Britain
by Amazon

51977760R00148